"L... ... Lainie,"

demanded Zachary, gripping her wrist.

Reacting to the threat in his voice, Lainie turned to him. "What?"

His green eyes narrowed. "Is this an act you're putting on for my benefit?"

"Don't flatter yourself, Zac. Now let go of my wrist."

"Not until I get a reaction out of you. Right now, I don't think you could care less if I dropped dead at your feet."

"Look, I'm not one of your little groupies, so don't expect me to act like one."

"Well, maybe you should. At least they get turned on to something. But not you. You're like a damn mannequin. Why don't you get angry or laugh or cry? I don't care. Just let me know you're alive in there. I want to see what makes you tick."

She tried to jerk free. "Well, it's not you, if that's what you think. So let go of my arm, Zachary. Now."

Dear Reader,

Welcome to Silhouette Romance—experience the magic of the wonderful world where two people fall in love. Meet heroines who will make you cheer for their happiness, and heroes (be they the boy next door or a handsome, mysterious stranger) who will win your heart. Silhouette Romance novels reflect the magic of love—sweeping you away with books that will make you laugh and cry, heartwarming, poignant stories that will move you time and time again.

In the next few months, we're publishing romances by many of your all-time favorites such as Diana Palmer, Brittany Young, Annette Broadrick and many others. Your response to these authors and other authors in Silhouette Romance has served as a touchstone for us, and we're pleased to bring you more books with Silhouette's distinctive medley of charm, wit and—above all—*romance*.

During 1991, we have many special events planned. Don't miss our WRITTEN IN THE STARS series. Each month in 1991, we're proud to present readers with a book that focuses on the hero—and his astrological sign.

I hope you'll enjoy this book and all of the stories to come. Come home to romance—Silhouette Romance—for always!

Sincerely,

Tara Gavin
Senior Editor

KRISTIN MORGAN

Love
Child

Silhouette *Romance*

Published by Silhouette Books New York

America's Publisher of Contemporary Romance

To Mom and Dad,
for teaching me to embrace life.
And to Sherwin, Julie, Lance
and Amy, for loving me.
I love you, too.

SILHOUETTE BOOKS
300 E. 42nd St., New York, N.Y. 10017

LOVE CHILD

ISBN: 0-373-08787-X

First Silhouette Books printing April 1991

All the characters in this book are fictitious. Any
resemblance to actual persons, living or dead, is
purely coincidental.

®: Trademark used under license and
registered in the United States Patent and
Trademark Office and in other countries.

Printed in the U.S.A.

KRISTIN MORGAN

lives in Lafayette, Louisiana, the very heart of Acadiana, where the French language of her ancestors is still spoken fluently by her parents and grandparents. Happily married to her high school sweetheart, she has three children whose ages range from eleven to twenty-four. She's traveled all over the South, as well as other areas of the United States and Mexico, with her husband, and they both count themselves lucky that their favorite city, New Orleans, is only two hours away from Lafayette.

In addition to her writing, she enjoys cooking and preparing authentic Cajun foods for her family with the recipies passed on to her through the generations. Her hobbies include reading—of course!—flower gardening and fishing. She loves walking in the rain, newborn babies, all kinds of music, chocolate desserts and love stories with happy endings. A true romantic at heart, she believes all things are possible with love.

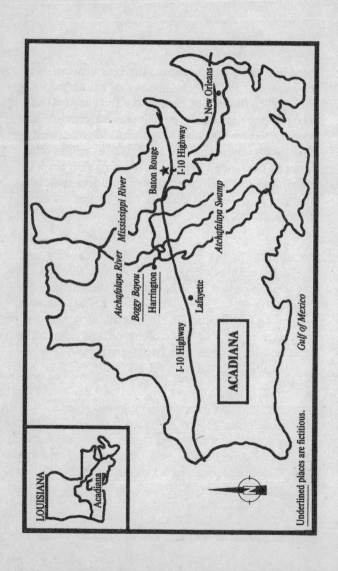

LOUISIANA

Acadiana

Mississippi River

Atchafalaya River

Boggy Bayou

Harrington

Baton Rouge

I-10 Highway

New Orleans

Lafayette

Atchafalaya Swamp

ACADIANA

I-10 Highway

Gulf of Mexico

N

Underlined places are fictitious.

Chapter One

The clock radio snapped on, and the lyrics to a country-and-western song drifted through the quiet of the early morning. Recognizing the artist, Lainie Benjamin's heart pounded like a tom-tom.

Fake. All his beautiful love songs were fake.

Tears stung the corners of her dark brown eyes as each strum of the steel guitar vibrated to some hidden part of her painful memories. She would never again let herself be fooled by the deep emotions Zachary Benjamin wove into every syllable. She was living proof he didn't mean one single word of the love songs he sang. Not one. Forcing down the lump in her throat, she swung her long shapely legs over the side of the bed and slid into a pair of blue cloth slippers.

The deejay's voice filled the room. "That was 'Give Me a Second Chance,' by the one and only Zachary Benjamin. It's his third number-one hit of the year. The guy just gets better with age. Did all you fans out there in

Cajunland know he'll celebrate his fortieth birthday in a couple of months? Well, so much for middle age."

And so much for fools like herself, Lainie thought.

She slipped into her robe without bothering to look at herself in the mirror over her dresser. After staring at the ceiling for most of the night, she didn't have any illusions about her appearance.

Damn Zachary and his telephone call last night. Just who did he think he was, phoning her after all this time? And just who the hell did he think he was, wanting to barge back into her life?

She walked into the bathroom, splashed cold water on her face and dabbed it dry with a towel. Then she looked in the mirror and grimaced.

What kind of a game was Zachary trying to play with her? If he really needed a rest like he'd said, then why not take a long vacation to some remote island? Lord knows, he had the money to do anything he wanted. Why come here?

"Why not?" he'd said when she'd asked him that very same question.

"Why not," indeed.

It just didn't make any sense to her. Not after twenty years. But then nothing made sense anymore. Not since Cory's death.

A piercing ache twisted its way deeper into her heart. Even after all this time, she couldn't think of Cory and Zachary in the same breath without all the anger and hurt she felt toward Zachary getting the better of her. And what of poor innocent Cory? She hated the way she'd gotten him caught up in her web of lies. He'd deserved so much more out of life. She took a deep breath, blinking back unshed tears.

Control was the key word here; she needed to get control of herself. She couldn't allow Zachary or anything he did to topple her composure. Her pride simply couldn't allow it. The seventeen-year-old girl he'd left behind twenty years ago didn't exist any longer. In her place was a strong-minded, independent woman who didn't need Zachary Benjamin anymore.

But no matter what she told herself, she still couldn't shake their conversation from the night before....

"Lainie, I need to come home for a while," he'd said.

Shocked, her response had been almost immediate. "Well...it's your house. I should've left when Cory died. I'll move out right away."

Not that she'd honestly wanted to do that. She belonged in this house. She and Cory had shared twenty years of marriage within these walls. Alyse, their daughter, had taken her first steps along its hallways. Though Cory was dead, and Alyse now attended college out of state, the house still whispered of the happy times they'd shared as a family. Every corner spoke of a lifetime of memories. Just because Zachary had decided to claim what was rightfully his didn't make it fair. This house and all its memories rightfully belonged to her.

"Look, Lainie," he'd said. "I have no intention of making you move out. I just need a short rest—away from it all. That old house is big. I'll stay out of your way, and I feel quite certain you'll stay out of mine." He'd hesitated and then said, "Am I right?"

"Well...yes—of course," she'd stammered like a fool. But then, wasn't that exactly what she was?

Why had he sounded so demanding—so caustic—when he'd said that? Had he been expecting her to put up a fight?

"Are you sure you want me to stay here while you're home?" she'd asked.

"Positive," he'd replied.

At first, she'd felt relieved. Then, after a while, she had begun to panic at the thought of the two of them alone under one roof. But that was before she reminded herself that she and Zac were history. What they'd shared as kids had meant nothing to him, and now it meant nothing to her.

So if he wanted to stay at the Benjamin house for a few weeks, she could hardly refuse him. After all, the house had belonged to his and Cory's parents. They'd left it to both boys, and now that Cory was dead, it was Zac's for the taking.

Their conversation had ended abruptly when he'd told her he would see her soon. How soon? she wondered as she brushed her teeth. She hadn't even had time to ask him before he'd hung up.

After gargling with mouthwash, she crushed the paper cup she'd used and tossed it into the wastebasket.

Well, she certainly didn't care when he showed up— and she certainly wasn't going to alter her life because of him. She had plans for the summer. Big plans.

What plans? her inner voice asked. She ignored it.

She swallowed, trying to get rid of the lump that had formed in her throat the moment she'd heard his voice.

I should have refused him, she thought, vividly recalling how he'd looked just the other night as she'd sat and watched his new music video on television. And *why* she'd watched that dumb thing, anyway, was still a mystery to her. Probably because there was nothing better on television. Yeah, she told herself. That was it. Summer reruns had begun.

For her own peace of mind, she hoped the deep tan and lean muscled body he'd displayed in the video had been just a trick of the camera and carefully applied makeup. If not, maturity had certainly graced him magnificently. She ignored the way her stomach quivered at the thought.

Her students' final test papers were stacked neatly on the bedside table. She had been working on them when Zachary telephoned. There were only two days left of school for this year, and for that she was grateful.

She'd hoped for a quiet summer, wanting to come to terms with a life without the presence of her husband and best friend. Cory was gone forever, and nothing she did today was going to change that. It was time to move on with her life. The trouble was, she didn't know in what direction she wanted to go.

Her daughter didn't need her anymore, at least, not like she once had. Alyse was almost a woman now, and it wouldn't be too much longer before she would go in search of her own dreams.

She and Cory had wanted other children, and now, more than ever, Lainie wished they'd had them. But she had never conceived again. The doctors finally told them they thought it was because Cory had a low sperm count.

Wasn't life strange? she thought. Once she would have sold her soul to have Zachary call to say he was coming home to her. Today it made her angry. Even worse, she was terrified of the consequences that could result. Nonetheless, it looked like now, instead of relaxing during the next few weeks as she'd planned to do, she would have to deal with his presence—and all the feelings she had pretended were long dead.

Her insides trembled at the idea of him being so near. What would Alyse think? And the townspeople? Dear God, how on earth was she going to handle this?

Readjusting the tie belt around her waist, she realized she needed to sit down and make plans, to take control of the situation. If she didn't, Zachary would find out just how much he'd hurt her all those years ago. And the one thing she remembered doing the day she married his younger brother, Cory, was promising herself that Zachary Benjamin would never know the truth. Thanks to Cory's unselfish nature, their reason for marrying so quickly had remained their secret.

She hurried down the stairs and into the kitchen. Soon the aroma of fresh coffee wafted up from the beige coffee maker next to the oven.

She rushed around the large room, its coziness enhanced by the smell that had seeped into the walls and ceiling from the apple-cinnamon pies that had been baked there over the years. She and Cory had intended to remodel his parents' old home, but they'd never gotten around to it. Now she was glad they hadn't. The door frame to the breakfast room still had the marks they'd made to show Alyse's height over the years, as well as those of Cory and Zachary. The tired-looking, off-white cabinets needed a new coat of paint, as did most of the old house. But Lainie wanted all those things to stay just as they were. With Cory gone, she needed the memories that went along with them.

She glanced at the clown-face clock, a result of one of Cory and Alyse's shopping sprees from years ago. So much had happened since then. She dropped into a nearby wooden dinette chair and waited for the coffee to finish brewing.

Cory's death had been such a shock. It still seemed like a nightmare, yet he was gone forever.

And now Zac was coming home.

Lainie leaned against the blue-and-white flowered wallpaper behind her and clasped her hands in her lap.

No matter how hard she tried to ignore it, she'd spent the last twenty years wanting to evict Zachary Benjamin from her heart. And she'd failed. But failing was one thing; letting him know was something else.

She worried about her daughter. Alyse wasn't a child any longer. What would she make of her famous uncle's visit? Would questions arise that were better left unanswered?

Where're your guts, Lainie? she argued with herself. No telling how much time you have to prepare for battle. Make use of every minute.

She filled her coffee mug and carried it upstairs so she could begin dressing for school. Her gaze fell on the wedding picture adorning the hallway wall. She didn't look much different than she had on that day. The few strands of gray in her light hair went undetected, and the small laugh lines along the corners of her eyes showed only when she smiled. At thirty-seven, she hadn't added an extra pound to her five-foot-eight frame. She and Cory had both thought it was important to stay in shape. The extra exercise had paid off for her, but all the special care in the world hadn't been enough to cure Cory. He'd died almost a year ago, just eighteen months after the doctors diagnosed his illness as cancer.

She walked into the bedroom and picked up the mahogany-framed photograph of her husband's family taken when Zac was sixteen and Cory fourteen. Their parents had died in an automobile accident soon after it was made. Their mother, Anna Alyse, had been a beautiful woman, with sable-brown hair and green eyes. Her dark, sensual looks had been passed on to her oldest son, Zac, and to her granddaughter. At nineteen, Alyse was the image of her grandmother, unlike Cory, who'd taken after his blond, gentle-looking father.

She replaced the photograph, sighed and turned to dress, knowing full well it wasn't going to be easy for her to handle Zachary. He had an irresistible charm that was almost sinful. He'd tempted her once, and she'd fallen into his trap. This time she had to be a lot smarter.

There was an old saying her daddy liked to use: "Once a fool, always a fool." Well, it was time she proved the opposite was just as true.

Lainie heard the two-thirty bell and realized she'd somehow made it through the day. The usual rowdiness the students demonstrated on the last days of school had only added to her restlessness. She'd spent the entire day fretting over Zac's phone call. A feeling of guilt forced her to listen with a smile as the junior class chattered about new clothes, the latest hair fashions and summer vacation.

She checked off a mental list of things to be done before she'd be ready to greet her uninvited guest. She needed to pick up her clothes from the cleaners. She needed to grocery shop and mow the grass. More importantly, she needed a new hairdo.

No, she thought suddenly, chastising herself. I most certainly am not going to change my hairstyle. Not for him.

Jarred into action when one of her students opened her classroom door, Lainie hastily ran the eraser across the blackboard. She was thankful she'd finished giving her English students their final exam yesterday.

Once again she was startled, this time by the sound of a metal trash can being kicked. She looked back.

"Lionel! Will you please stop making so much noise! I asked you to empty the trash can, not play the drums." Snickers graduated into peels of laughter. Lainie's head began to throb. She glanced at the wall clock.

"Class dismissed. Now, please go quietly and wait in the front lobby for the last bell."

The students jumped up and scrambled toward the door. She returned her attention to the blackboard with a slow shake of her head. Almost immediately, she heard loud screams and shrieks coming from the front of the building. She expected someone to run in to say one of the boys had placed some sort of weird creature in one of the girl's lockers, but when no one did and the squeals continued, Lainie walked toward the disturbance. She'd reached her classroom door when a female student, whose clothing resembled castoffs from an old Dracula movie, came screaming down the hallway. Flabbergasted as to the reason for such a display, Lainie followed her.

In the main lobby, a large group of teenage girls crowded around a tall, broad-shouldered man with a white Western hat on his head, each girl pushing to get closer to him. Lainie stopped at a distance, frowning at the confusion. It couldn't be....

Just then, a friend and colleague, Debra Cohen, walked up beside her. "What's going on?" she asked, but before Lainie could answer, she heard Debra's intake of breath.

"My God! That's Zachary Benjamin!" Debra exclaimed. She turned suddenly, her eyes round with excitement, and tugged at Lainie's arm. "That's your brother-in-law! Oh—Lainie, he's probably here to see you. How exciting!"

"Damn," Lainie said. No wonder the whole student body had converged in the main lobby. Suddenly all the voices sounded as if they were echoing in a barrel. The throbbing in her head intensified. She needed more time.

Lainie stood transfixed for a couple of seconds, then turned and started to flee for the safety of her classroom. But above all the din she heard her name being called. She froze, and an immediate quiet filled the lobby. She turned slowly, determined to keep a tight rein on her chaotic thoughts.

There were low murmurs as the students parted, making an open path between her and Zac. In four long graceful strides he stood within a few feet of her, and for one timeless second his light emerald eyes pinned her to the place where she stood. The sheer power he exuded seeped into her every pore. Every nerve in her body came alive. She felt as though she were being consumed.

"Lainie, you look surprised to see me," he drawled in the deep Southern accent that made each word sound like a song. He grinned down at her, his even white teeth gleaming in contrast to his deep olive complexion. A resurrected emotion she was forced to acknowledge tugged at her heart. The realization that she still loved him so much scared her. She felt a kind of danger, a certain challenge, in the depths of his knowing eyes. Her breath locked in her throat. *He can't possibly know how I feel,* she thought. It had been a lifetime since they'd even spoken such words to each other.

"You didn't say when you'd be coming, and I—I certainly didn't expect to see you here," she replied quickly.

His grin was seductive as he tucked his fingertips in the back pockets of his fitted bootcut jeans. "Well, don't get so flustered up. I arrived a little earlier than I thought I would, so I decided to see if the old high school still looked the same. But if it'll make you happy, I càn leave."

"I—"

The students' renewed excitement swallowed up her next words. She thought it was just as well. They wouldn't have made any more sense than her previous ones. She was completely ignored by the students descending on Zac, waving scraps of paper for autographs. Lainie backed away and was thankful for the few extra minutes she'd been given to collect her thoughts.

He's a charmer, she thought, watching the ease with which he handled the crowd. The clean-cut appearance, short hair, shaven face and crisp white pin-striped shirt were part of his masculine appeal. His high cheekbones and straight Anglo-Saxon nose only accented the most beautiful green eyes Lainie had ever gazed into. Alyse had those same eyes. Lainie recalled her daughter's emerald depths and wanted to cry. Sometimes those green pools became too much of a reminder.

Lainie closed her classroom door behind her and leaned against it for a brief moment. A woman would have to be blind or frozen not to be affected by Zac's charisma. Lainie knew just how easily a girl could fall in love with him. She had. And he'd been only a skinny, good-looking kid of nineteen at the time. Now he was a man, experienced and aware of his ability, making him as dangerous as a hurricane brewing in the Gulf of Mexico. In order to survive, she knew she needed to harden her heart and prepare herself for the turbulent days ahead.

The few minutes she'd hoped to have to herself dragged into thirty. The last of the school buses were departing. The noise in the hallway had lessened. In spite of herself, she kept glancing toward the closed classroom door, knowing Zachary would be coming through it at any time. She cleared her desk, then walked to the window and stared out.

She'd started her junior year of high school here in Harrington after her parents moved from Beaumont to this small country town in south Louisiana. She and Cory Benjamin had shared several classes and, as a result, they'd become immediate friends. Lainie had liked his quiet manner, and Cory had taken a personal interest in helping her adjust to the new school.

Cory had been like that—unselfish, always helping her when she'd needed a friend. In the end, when Lainie knew he was going to die, she'd done everything she could to help him. Tears filled her eyes. God, but she missed him. Cory had been her husband, but, more importantly, he'd been her best friend. And she'd loved him for it. Lainie thanked God every day for those years when Cory had stood by her and loved her despite everything.

She heard a light knock just before the door opened. Feeling the dread of a convicted prisoner awaiting sentencing, she turned to face Zachary. Her body trembled slightly. Dampness formed in the palms of her hands, and her heart began to pound.

She wondered if Zachary had any idea how his presence affected her. Did he realize she still remembered the feel of his naked body pressed against hers? If he did, he gave no indication of it as he casually surveyed the classroom before resting his appraising eyes on her face.

"You look great, Lainie. Marriage must have agreed with you," he said, allowing his hot gaze to travel the length of her. "You're every bit as beautiful as I remember."

A red hue crept up Lainie's neck and settled along the fine planes of her face. Willing her mind and body to remain in control, she attempted to shrug off his compliment. "You're looking well, too. Fame agrees with *you*."

Zachary flashed a liquid grin. "Do you really think so?"

"Yes, of course. I wouldn't have said so if I didn't."

"It sure has taken you a long time to get around to saying it."

"Well, I certainly wasn't going to go chasing you around the world."

"I thought they made telephones for such things," he answered.

"Apparently that's something you just found out for yourself," she shot back.

He shrugged. "So now what? Are we going to fight the entire time I'm here?"

She could think of worse things for them to be doing. "Of course not." She cleared her throat. "Well, are you overworked? I mean, is that why you need a rest?"

"Yeah, you might say that," he drawled, deliberately not giving her a direct answer. "I decided I ought to take advantage of the moment and come home for a while. It was time, don't you think?"

The intensity of his heated gaze almost shattered her composure. Ignoring his question, she turned, picked up the stack of books on the end of her desk and grabbed her purse in the same motion. She wasn't about to stand here and have a personal conversation with him. She wasn't prepared for that. Not yet. "I'm ready to leave if you are. Did you drive your own car or come by limo?"

Hooking his thumbs in his belt loops, Zachary tossed her a lopsided grin. "I drove."

Lainie wondered if he felt as ill at ease with her as she did with him. If so, he certainly wasn't letting it show. He looked every bit as self-assured as she remembered. She struggled for something light to say, but nothing came to mind. Too many unanswered questions were bouncing around inside her head, but now wasn't the time to bombard him with questions that might have lengthy answers. All she wanted was to get home and prepare her own defense against all the disturbing feelings churning inside her.

She wondered momentarily if he'd planned this visit or if it had been a sudden whim. Whatever it was, it had certainly thrown her life into chaos. Somehow, though, she had a feeling he couldn't have cared less if his temporary presence in her life bothered her. He'd changed—a lot—and that, too, scared her. The tiny lines along the corners of his eyes told her that life had placed its mark upon him, as well. He was much more...arrogant—and cynical, too, she thought. But what in heaven's name did he have to be cynical about? Hadn't the years brought him everything life had to offer on a silver platter?

She started to walk past him, but he stepped into her path. Her breath locked in her throat, and it took her a moment to squelch the panic swelling in her chest.

"Yes?" she questioned, keeping her eyes level with the V of his open collar. Her mouth dried at the sight of the dark curly hair that sprang from the opening. She started to inhale deeply of his clean scent but forced her breathing to remain even.

"Lainie, I can tell you're not very happy about this arrangement."

She kept her eyes focused on the dark buttons of his shirt. "It doesn't bother me any."

"Lainie, would you look at me when I talk to you?" Zac said, placing his index finger under her chin and lifting her face. His gaze wandered over her strained features, causing her knees to weaken. From her naturally arched brows to the full lips that she unconsciously moistened with her tongue, his emerald gaze pored over her face, heating her skin like liquid fire before coming to rest on her quivering mouth. His fingers stretched out along her jawline, and for one timeless moment twenty years slipped away.

She remembered the touch of his long, smooth fingers from those lazy summer nights so long ago when he'd promised to love her forever.

Suddenly she jerked back. Zachary frowned, his eyes narrowing as he spoke. "Hey, look, can't we be friends, at least for the time being?"

His words rang in her ears. "Friends?" Lainie laughed. "I thought we already were."

Zachary shook his head, indicating he knew she really didn't feel that way. "I knew this wasn't going to be easy on either of us, but I didn't expect you to be so uptight. What's your problem? Are you afraid of something? Of me?"

A slap in the face wouldn't have stunned her more. Afraid? Yes, she was afraid. "Don't be absurd," she said defensively. "It's just that after all these years, we're like two strangers, that's all."

A loud knock on the door interrupted them. Debra Cohen beamed as she strolled into the room, her eyes glued on Zachary.

Grateful for the intrusion, Lainie seized the opportunity. "Zachary, this is Debra Cohen, a friend of mine."

Debra's attempt to act normal failed. She looked just as awed as the students had earlier. "This is so exciting. You know, it's not every day that Zachary Benjamin just walks into his hometown school." She giggled like one of her students. "I'm sure you don't remember me. I was five years younger than you."

"No, I don't. But then, you were still a kid when I left."

Debra smiled. "Well, I'm all grown-up now."

"You sure are," Zachary drawled.

"Are you here for a visit?"

"I guess you could say I'm here for both business and pleasure," Zac replied easily, giving Debra his poster-perfect smile.

"Are you planning to stay awhile?"

His eyes shifted to Lainie. "That depends. I might be."

"Great! Maybe you and Lainie could come over for... for a party, or dinner... or something."

Zac grinned. "Sounds good to me. But you'll have to ask my sister-in-law."

"Lainie?"

"Uuuh... yeah, sounds great," Lainie said. She couldn't believe what was happening.

She felt as though she was losing control over her well-organized life. She liked schedules, and even during Cory's illness, she'd managed to keep their lives running smoothly. Yet in just a few minutes Zachary had disrupted hers to the point that she couldn't even think straight.

She walked briskly to the door, then turned before stepping into the hallway and spoke to Zachary. "There's still a key to the house hidden in the same place as always. Do you remember?" She waited for his brief, self-assured nod. "Good. I've got several errands to run. I'll see you at the house later." Exiting, she didn't wait for his reply and ignored her friend's stunned expression.

Outside, she scanned the parking lot as she headed for her car. A brand-new white Jaguar parked next to hers left little doubt as to its owner. As far as Lainie knew, no one in Harrington drove a Jag, least of all the principal of the school whose space it occupied.

The sun reflected off the shiny finish. She forgot her hurry and walked around the sports car, noting in detail its unique design, its royal-blue interior. How many times had she commented that if she were ever wealthy enough, she'd drive a white Jaguar?

From the corner of her eye, she saw Zachary step up behind her.

"Like it?"

"Of course. I'd have to be blind not to," Lainie replied, still gazing at the automobile. "Besides, what's not to love about a white sports car, especially a Jaguar? They're my favorite."

"Really?"

Detecting a curious note in his voice, Lainie slowly turned to face him. Zac held the keys in midair, dangling them between his thumb and index finger. He grinned like a child giving his teacher a wildflower picked along the way to school.

"Here. You drive it," he said, sounding pleased with himself. "I'll take your car home."

Lainie's heart stopped between beats. He'd used the word *home* so easily. But of course it *was* his home—or at least it had been until he'd left it to pursue a singing career that blossomed into stardom. Did it seem strange to him, coming back after all these years? Lainie weighed the keys, the Jag and Zachary's smiling face. For just a moment she thought of driving the sports car, but then she told herself not to be crazy, to keep her distance.

Shading her eyes from the sun's glare, she said, "No, I can't. The whole town will be talking if I zoom around picking up groceries and laundry in a car like that."

"Since when do you care what anyone says? The Lainie I remember would've laughed in their faces."

"Well, I'm older now, and I have to live here. Have you forgotten what it's like living in a small community?"

She felt defensive. Sure, when she was a rebellious teenager, she'd laughed in the face of tradition. Who hadn't, in those days? But now, as a high school teacher and member of the parish board, her life had settled into a routine similar to the other citizens of Harrington. And it was a good life, without glamour and glitz, but filled with good friends and good memories. How dare he come back here after all these years and complain because she'd changed!

Zac stretched out his hands in front of him. "Hey, look, don't get upset. I didn't mean anything by it. Small towns are great. They're the backbone of country music."

Lainie spoke over her shoulder as she marched to her own car and unlocked the door. "Good. Just remember, I have to live in this town—you don't." She got in, started the motor and drove away without looking back at him, but the superior feeling she'd aimed for failed to come. Instead, she felt like an oversensitive fool.

With his hands on his hips, his feet spread apart and a frown etched across his face, Zachary watched her drive away. For a second there, he'd wanted to call her back and apologize.

And that was what had him so astounded with himself. He had only one reason for being in Harrington, and that was to make Lainie Benjamin pay for all her treachery. During the last months he'd lain awake night after night scheming to get even with her, waiting for the time to be right, and now that he was here, he couldn't wait to tell her in so many words just what he thought of her cheating ways, not to mention the fact that she'd never told him about their child. Revenge was going to be as sweet as honey. He planned to seduce her with false words of love until she was at her most vulnerable. Then he would tell her that he'd set her up, and her complete mortification at what he'd done to her would be his triumph—and rightfully so, he told himself. It was only fair that she should pay.

But that, he realized, wasn't going to be as easily accomplished as he'd thought. Lainie *had* changed. She wasn't the naive girl he'd kept in his heart all these years, and the slight quivering in the pit of his stomach told him that the woman she'd become was having a strong effect on him.

Ignoring it, he turned around and gazed at the high school building that once had been such a big part of his life. He sighed heavily.

Why were his thoughts of revenge failing to seem as sweet as they had a few months ago? Even a week ago?

He was just rattled from seeing Lainie after all this time. Hadn't he known she would have an effect on him? Sure, but what he hadn't counted on was the explosion she'd caused inside him.

So if you're gonna be the mean SOB you came here to be, tighten up, Benjamin. Only a fool would let a woman like her work her way back into your heart.

That thought jarred him into action. He headed for his car, assuring himself that he most certainly wasn't going to let that happen. Damn her lying ways. No amount of money and fame could buy back what she'd stolen from him. He was just thankful he'd made it to his brother's bedside in time to understand Cory's nearly incoherent ramblings. Otherwise, Zac realized, he would never have known that Alyse was really his child. It was apparent that Lainie had had no intention of telling him.

His grin was wicked as he slid into his car. Oh, he planned on smiling at her and saying the nice things he needed to say, but he wouldn't forget for one moment his goal in being here. And in order to reaffirm his ability to pull off his plan, he repeated to himself his promise of revenge.

Plain and simple, Zachary Benjamin was home to even the score.

Chapter Two

Lainie carried in her first load of groceries and quietly closed the door to the house as she headed once again to the car. She wished she had a carport connected to the house instead of a garage seventy-five feet away, especially when it was cold or raining—or both.

It had taken forever to complete her errands. Word of Zachary's appearance at Harrington High had spread through town like mosquitoes on a hot, humid evening. Everyone wanted to know his plans, and as Lainie tried to explain them, she found herself wondering the same thing. Just what *were* his plans now that he was back in town?

On the way home she'd finally had to ask herself if maybe she wasn't blowing this whole thing out of proportion. After all, maybe it was normal of him to want to come home. And, too, just maybe she'd become too concerned with the opinions of other people, as she'd often accused her friends of doing.

"See," she argued aloud while grabbing more grocery bags from the trunk of her car, "Zac already has me questioning myself."

There had been no lights on, no signs of life in the big house, and she wondered if he was asleep, and if so, in which bedroom he had settled. The house contained only three: the master suite, which she used; Cory's old room, which had been renovated for Alyse; and Zachary's old bedroom. Reason told her that he'd probably settled into his old room, but what if he'd decided he wanted the master suite? She almost felt like laughing at herself, the thought was so stupid, and yet she knew there wasn't a darn thing funny about the situation.

They would have to share the only upstairs bathroom, which was across the hall from her room and filled with all her toiletries and personal things. How on earth were they going to handle that?

And what would they say to each other when they were alone, which she realized would be practically all the time?

The hostility and suspicion she felt toward him were justified, she told herself. After all, not only had he lied about his promise to come back for her all those years ago, but he'd left her pregnant, without any concern for her or the baby she carried. She'd had no choice but to keep the truth from him, right?

Right.

Absorbed in her thoughts, she screamed when she felt an arm reach from behind her. "Zachary! You scared the daylights out of me! I thought you were inside, asleep."

"I'm sorry," Zac said, sounding sincere. He stood just behind her, and suddenly his nearness became a much bigger problem for her than his abrupt appearance. "I got up about thirty minutes ago and decided to walk along Boggy. You know, that old bayou hasn't changed a bit.''

"Like I said, things around here don't change much," Lainie said, turning to face him, her arms loaded with groceries. Zachary took the heavy bags from her as he glanced into the trunk.

"Are you planning a party or just feeding an army?"

Her smile became fixed on her face when she noticed he'd removed his shirt. She swallowed hard, and it sounded to her like a tin pail being dropped in a well.

"I hate to grocery shop for just me, so I always put it off till the last minute," she said, relieved that her voice hadn't trembled as she'd spoken. But no matter how much she wanted to look away, she couldn't pull her gaze from his muscled torso glistening in the late-afternoon heat.

Noting the dark hair that covered his chest and traveled down his taut, flat stomach, disappearing beneath his low-riding jeans, she felt heat rising in her. As far as she could tell, he didn't have a tan line around his waist. Maybe if his jeans rode his hips a bit lower....

The memory of some movie actress commenting that Zac had the sexiest chest she'd ever seen caused Lainie to tremble. That had been years ago, while she'd been recuperating from Alyse's birth. She recalled crying for hours, thinking about his making love to another woman. But looking back now, she realized the woman hadn't actually said they were having an affair. She had only commented that his chest was a tempting, seductive view of masculinity at its best. Suddenly Lainie found herself wondering if she hadn't drawn the wrong conclusion—though the whole thing and how she'd felt about it at the time were totally irrelevant to her now.

She suddenly realized she was staring. Her eyes darted in another direction.

Thank God he hadn't seemed to notice because she sure didn't have a sane excuse to give him if he had.

"I think it's kind of nice the way things stay the same around here," he was saying, shifting the grocery bags in his arms. "The rest of the world changes enough as it is." He turned and looked directly into her eyes. "How about you, Lainie? Deep down inside, has the lovely little songbird of my youth changed?"

Her insides tightened like the strings of a bass guitar. She hesitated before answering him, but when at last she did, the sudden anger she felt was evident in her voice. "Yes, I've changed. I'm not a child anymore."

Zachary's eyes roamed over her. "I've noticed. Some things do get better with age."

His earlier use of the pet name he'd given her years ago had left her insides rattling like a glass building in the middle of an earthquake. She turned quickly, grabbed the last bag and slammed the trunk. When she turned to face him again, there was a sudden determination written on her face.

"I think I need to say something, and it's best to say it right off. What happened between us is over—has been over for twenty years." Lainie felt adrenaline pumping through her veins as his face shone with amusement at her outburst. "And just what is so damn funny?"

"I knew the old Lainie was in there somewhere. I couldn't believe you'd changed completely. I was right. The old fire I remember just sparked in your eyes."

"The old fire was smothered years ago, Zac. What you just saw was a spark of frustration. But you're right about one thing. I *am* unhappy about your coming here, and I really don't understand why you felt it was neces-

sary. Could you answer that one question for me?
Why?"

He shrugged. "You wouldn't believe me if I told you,
Lainie," he said, his voice losing all humor. "Let's just
say it's very important to me, sort of a matter of life and
death."

Lainie's heart pounded in her chest. "Are you sick?"

"In a way," he answered, his expression impassive.

He turned and headed into the house. Lainie followed
right behind, bewildered by his reply.

"What kind of an answer is that? In *what* way?"

He whirled around to face her, his arms loaded with
groceries. Lainie halted just inches from crashing into
him.

"Look, I need a rest. No big deal, just a rest. I've
needed one for a long time, but it was impossible to come
home until now." Suddenly his expression changed, and
he sniffed in one of the bags. "What smells so good?"

"Huhh...? Oh—it must be the French bread. It was
still piping hot when I picked it up," Lainie said. "Is that
the only answer you're going to give me?"

"Yep." Zac closed his eyes and sniffed again. "Man,
when do we eat?"

She tried not to smile, but this lighter side of him was
contagious. Her heart sang with unexpected pleasure at
the idea of preparing a meal for a man's hungry appe-
tite. It had been so long....

"I'm making a potato casserole. Along with steak and
salad, that ought to do it," she said, pulling groceries out
of the bags and putting them away.

"And wine."

She whirled around at the comment. She'd bought the
wine on a whim and hadn't intended for Zachary to know
it had been purchased just today. But now that he'd seen

it, there wasn't much she could do. She laughed lightly while searching for something to say.

"Cory always said we couldn't have grilled steak without a bottle of wine to complement the taste. It's become a habit with me."

"Nice habit," Zac replied. He returned his interest to the groceries and started to empty the bag. "You miss him a lot, don't you?"

Lainie stopped what she was doing. She hadn't expected the question—not yet.

"I miss him terribly. He was a wonderful friend—and husband. I loved him very much."

"I loved him, too."

Lainie felt the depth of his sadly spoken words. She glanced back.

Zac stood with his back to her as he unpacked the last two grocery bags. Her eyes were drawn to the lean muscles flexing along his shoulders as he went about his task. Everything about him caught her eye, and she hated herself for it. Just the way he breathed seemed to affect her.

"He was very proud of you," she said, for lack of something better. "He always said you'd make it to the top. He was right."

Tears filled her eyes as she returned to stacking the canned goods in the pantry. Cory's devotion to his older brother was hard to explain. Even though he, too, had been angry with Zac in the beginning, over the years he had learned to forgive him and had tried his best to get Lainie to do the same. But that was Cory's way of loving. He always looked for the good in everyone. "I thank God for so many happy memories . . . all the years of laughter . . . this house he loved. . . ."

"How about your daughter?"

A stifling heat penetrated her body, and she trembled at his reference to her daughter. Did he suspect something? Was he deliberately doing this to her?

Dear God, she should have realized something like this was coming. Please, she prayed, don't let me lose control. Not now, when it means so much to say the right thing.

"Of course—Alyse, too. I . . . I just wasn't thinking along those lines. Cory adored her, and she worshiped the ground he walked on. Their relationship was very special."

Her mind flooded with bittersweet memories—memories of Cory tossing Alyse in the air, tucking her in at bedtime. He'd been a wonderful father. The love and patience he'd given Alyse were special. That was another of the reasons why she thanked God daily.

"Well," Zac said, sounding cynical, "sounds to me like the three of you were the all-American family."

Frowning, Lainie glanced in his direction. His jaw was clenched tight. He looked angry or frustrated, or both. What in the world had him so upset? she wondered, but she didn't ask, because she didn't know if she really wanted to hear the answer.

He completed emptying the last paper bag, wadded it up and threw it in the wastebasket. "Well, at least you didn't change the inside of the house much. I wondered about that. I'm glad to see it's still pretty much the same."

Lainie looked at him for another second before glancing nervously around the room. She was glad the subject of her daughter had been dropped, and happy to see he was talking again, though the catch she'd heard in his voice worried her.

"We often thought about remodeling, but other things always got in the way. Schoolteachers don't make a lot of money. We were just beginning to accumulate a small savings account when Cory got sick, and most of what we had was gone in a short while."

"I wished I'd known sooner," he said. "Why didn't you call me the moment you found out he had cancer? Didn't you think I would have cared?"

Lainie took a deep breath and drummed up every ounce of courage she had. She turned to face him. "Why should we have thought that? We hadn't heard a word from you in about twenty years. Not one word. Not even so much as a Christmas card."

"Oh, no," he said, just as forceful as she had been. "Don't give me that lousy excuse about no word from me, because I can say the same thing about you." His face became flushed. "I didn't even rate an invitation to your wedding."

Lainie felt breathless. "We didn't send invitations."

"Don't play games with me, Lainie. You know what I'm talking about."

"Look," she said, licking her dry lips, "I would have called you . . . at the end, if Alyse hadn't taken it on herself to do it."

At the time, her daughter had had no way of knowing that her parents had made a decision to wait until the very end before contacting her uncle. That meant less time spent in Zachary's company, less time for unwanted questions. "I know I thanked you at the funeral for the money, and we haven't spoken since, except for last night, but I want you to know I plan on paying you back as soon as I can."

Zachary charged across the kitchen and imprisoned her against the cabinet before she had a chance to utter another word. Leaning into her face, he said, "Don't you ever say that again. I gave you that money for my brother's care. He deserved the best. So let's drop the subject."

His forcefulness astounded her, and her heart began a frantic pounding. The heat from his body inflamed her every nerve. He'd wanted to make a point, and he had. Now all she wanted was for him to move away. His nearness caused her body to react in ways that had nothing to do with anything but her own need to be held close by those strong arms.

He stepped closer, forcing her snugly between him and the kitchen sink. A light flared in the depths of his emerald eyes. He stared boldly at her mouth, and Lainie felt her breathing become short gasps as it mingled with his. Her mind whirled between wanting to be kissed and wanting to turn and run. He leaned his head closer, and his mouth descended toward hers. Her indecision gave way to a moan, and she tried to run. But Zac extended his arm, blocking her way. His other hand tunneled through her silky hair and held her head in place.

"No, Zac. Please don't," she said, her voice quivering with emotion. If their lips touched, Lainie knew she would explode into tiny pieces. Every nerve in her body begged for his touch, but she was determined to deny her need.

Zac's body stilled as he fought for control. Lainie fought the desire to throw caution away and allow each moment to take care of itself.

She'd be sorry tomorrow, she told herself.

She wasn't sure just what his game was—or if, indeed, it was a game. Cory had told her through the years that Zachary wasn't like that. That he was honest, true. But everything that had happened from the time he left her with a promise to return until she'd married Cory, proved otherwise. She remembered the pain of rejection when he didn't answer her phone calls. For two weeks she'd tried desperately to reach him. She'd left messages everywhere. Young, pregnant and alone, she'd panicked by the time Cory came to her rescue and assumed total responsibility for her unborn child. The truth of Alyse's conception remained a secret shared by only her and her husband. Zac hadn't cared what happened to her, and she didn't feel he deserved the truth. Ever. She'd be a fool to trust him again, and the future of her secret depended on her keeping a cool, level head—and a hardened heart, as well.

As abruptly as he'd pinned her there, Zac suddenly dropped his arms, turned and walked out of the kitchen. Lainie heard his footsteps on the stairs, and she breathed a sigh of relief. She wasn't prepared for a confrontation with him tonight. She doubted if she ever would be.

Zac went straight to his room, lay across the bed and placed his forearm over his eyes. Every nerve inside of him was alive with feeling: anger, frustration, disappointment—and yes, desire. Lainie had looked so vulnerable that he'd almost lost control and kissed her. What had him so confused was that he felt sure that just a little more coaxing on his part and she would have been willing. So why hadn't he taken advantage of the moment? Wasn't seducing her part of his carefully laid-out plan?

But he hadn't counted on feeling like this. How could she get to him like that? Why couldn't he just carry out each calculated move and, in due time, put the screws to her the way she deserved?

He thought about Cory, and tears stung in his eyes. He
had made a big mistake where his brother was concerned. He should have stayed in touch with him—not
with Lainie, but with Cory. Once they had been close,
and though Cory hadn't tried to keep in touch, either,
that, too, was probably because of Lainie. Now Zac felt
he should have been the one to step over the imaginary
boundaries that had somehow been drawn between them.
Instead he'd taken the coward's way out by staying away,
and he'd lost his brother in the process. That was another reason to hate Lainie, not that he really needed
more than he already had.

She wasn't going to get off so easily this time, though.
Just because she looked at him with those big, brown eyes
of hers, and just because his libido was in overdrive,
didn't mean a thing. So what if he had the hots for her?
It would just make it easier for him to seduce her.

His plan was working out perfectly, just perfectly.

"Can I help?" Zachary asked, entering the kitchen an
hour later, wearing a solid navy blue jogging suit, complete with leather sneakers.

At first glance Lainie knew he had just stepped out of
the shower, because his dark hair glistened with mois-
ture. She slid the potato casserole into the oven.

Well, she quickly decided, if he could so easily dis-
pense with the earlier episode between them, then she
could, too.

"Actually, I was thinking of having a glass of wine.
Maybe you could get the bottle out of the fridge."

"Sure. Got something to open it with?"

"In there," she replied, pointing toward the counter.

Zachary pulled open a drawer and dug through all the
cooking utensils until he found what he was looking for.

Lainie hated the way her eyes kept drifting in his direction as she sliced cucumbers for the salad. And even worse, she hated the way her heart fluttered each time she saw him.

"So...tell me what it feels like to be a superstar," she said hesitantly, after frantically searching her brain for a topic of discussion. She had never had so much trouble carrying on a conversation with anyone.

He continued his task. "What is there to say? It's rewarding in a lot of ways. The offers pour in. Record contracts. Commercials. Movie offers. And the money's not bad, either. Where are the wineglasses?"

"Oh—right here," she said, stopping what she was doing to get them out of the cabinet. "I guess things worked out for you just like you planned all along."

Zachary looked at her oddly, almost accusingly. "No, not quite everything."

Well, it was your decision to leave Harrington, she thought, avoiding his overheated gaze. Nothing had been important enough, strong enough, to stop him. Not even their love. Singing his songs had been like a disease—and stardom had been the only cure. Lainie realized that now.

Popping the cork from the bottle of wine, he said, "I try to jog every day, but I was thinking of getting in some extra exercise while I'm here. Care to play a game of tennis tomorrow?"

Lainie raised her eyebrows in surprise. "You still play tennis?"

"I didn't for a long time."

Carrying the chilled wine, he walked up beside her and filled the two crystal goblets she had placed on the cabinet. "But, to be perfectly honest, I've been practicing every chance I get for the last couple of weeks, just in case I could talk you into a match. I didn't want to look like a slob out on the court. I have a perfect record to defend.''

Lainie's expression went blank. "I don't ever remember you beating me in a game of tennis."

Grinning, he said, "See what I mean?"

Her immediate response to his request was to match his grin and say yes, but then she frowned. "I can't—not tomorrow." And then, almost in the same breath, she said, "Did you say you'd been practicing for a couple of weeks? So you *had* been planning this visit for some time. Care to tell me why you didn't bother to inform me until last night?"

He placed the bottle of wine back in the refrigerator. "I admit I've been thinking about it for a while, but all of a sudden things just sort of fell into place at the last minute." He turned to face her. "Did my sudden arrival create a problem for you?"

"Yes—no—well, not exactly. I just wish you'd called sooner."

Leaning against the counter next to her, he sipped his wine. "What would you have done differently if I'd called sooner?"

His question startled her. "Well, I don't know. But a little more warning would have helped."

"Warning, huh? Is that how you think of my coming home?"

"No—of course not. I didn't mean it like that. It's just that after all these years I would have made sure you weren't disappointed, that's all."

He moved closer. "Stop worrying. I'm not disappointed. Not in the least."

"Yes, but the lawn needs mowing. I could have had it cut if I'd known."

He looked amused. "Are we really talking about grass here?"

"Of course," she replied nervously, her throat feeling as if it were closing up on her. "What else?"

"You."

"I'd rather talk about grass."

"I'd rather talk about you."

"Zachary..."

"Okay. So I'll mow the lawn while I'm here. Does that make you feel better?"

"You don't have to do that. I usually hire someone."

"I want to. It'll be relaxing—and a way of getting that extra exercise I won't be getting on the court tomorrow."

"Maybe one of your old friends would like to play a game with you. Why don't you call one of them?"

He lifted a strand of her hair and rubbed it between his long fingers. The heat of his body threatened her. "I wanted to play with you," he said smoothly. "We had some good times together, just you and me. I'd like to have them again, wouldn't you?"

She couldn't find her voice to answer him. His hot, sultry breath near her face had swept it away.

He dropped the first lock of hair and picked up another. The fine hair along the back of her neckline tingled with awareness.

"Remember all those hours we spent along Boggy Bayou? I'd strum my guitar, and you'd make up the lyrics to go along with my music?"

Lainie's hands began to shake. She hesitated before answering, hoping her words would make sense. "It was so long ago, Zac. I've forgotten all that stuff."

He didn't answer her, but she could feel his gaze on her face. Her attempt at buttering the French bread was a loss. Taking a slow, deep breath, she stopped what she was doing and stared straight ahead. "Why have you come home, Zac?"

Several silent moments passed. "Why do you think?" he asked, the huskiness in his voice turning her insides to mush and pushing her control nearer to the edge.

"I don't know," she answered breathlessly.

"I'm only human, Lainie. I needed to come back to my roots for a while." He hesitated before continuing. "Don't you ever have a sudden need to do something?"

"Of course I have needs," she replied anxiously.

"Why don't you tell me a few?" Zac asked, his voice warm against her cheek. He was so close now that if she'd turned her head to face him, their noses would have touched.

She could almost taste the tension of the moment.

"I don't think that's necessary," she said, scrambling around in her brain for a strong answer. Unfortunately, she didn't find one.

"Come on," he said in that smooth voice of his that was probably insured for more money than she could earn in a lifetime. "It's not easy to get along when only one of us is trying to bridge the gap between us. Let's be friends. After all, we're family, aren't we?"

She felt his fingers filtering through her hair once more. Shaken by his voice, his nearness and his unknown motive for doing what he was doing, she lifted her hand to stop him. "Look, I've cooperated with you from the moment you telephoned. What more do you want?" she asked.

He gripped her wrist in midair. "Look at me, Lainie."

Defying his command, she gazed straight ahead.

"Lainie, I said look at me."

Reacting to the threat in his voice, she turned her eyes to him. "What?"

His green eyes narrowed. "Is this act you're putting on for my benefit?"

"Don't flatter yourself, Zac. Now let go of my wrist."

"Not until I get a reaction out of you. Right now, I don't think you could care less if I dropped dead at your feet."

"Look, I'm not one of your little groupies, so don't expect me to act like one."

"Well, maybe you should. At least they get turned on to something. But not you. You're like a damn mannequin. Why don't you get angry or laugh or cry— Hell! I don't care. Just let me know you're alive in there. I want to see what makes you tick."

She tried to jerk free. "Well, it's not you, if that's what you think. Now let go of my arm, Zachary. Now."

"I don't think I will. At least you're showing signs of emotion. I was beginning to think you didn't have any."

She tried to break free again, and this time he let her. Breathing as if she'd just finished a marathon, she picked up the salad, walked to the refrigerator and set it inside. Then she turned to face him. "Don't you ever touch me again. Not ever."

Zachary moved away from the counter he'd been leaning against. He walked straight toward her. "And just what makes you think I'd want to waste the time?"

With that he strolled right passed her and out the door, letting it slam behind him. Angered and shaken to the point of tears, Lainie stared after him. When he stopped to pet her dog, Morris, on the head, she saw him glance back toward the house. She quickly turned away.

Damn him. This was the last time he was going to get the better of her—ever.

Chapter Three

The early-morning sun slowly eased itself above the horizon as Zachary strolled across the backyard, thinking about dinner the previous night. The meal had gone fairly well—not quite as well as he'd wanted, but then, he realized he'd probably hoped for too much. The conversation had consisted of idle chitchat. The night had ended when Lainie had suddenly announced that she was going up to bed. What could he have said to that? No, don't leave yet. Wait—I'll go with you. He'd thought of doing just that.

The rays from the sun felt warm on his face as he stared into the sky, watching a crow soar by. Bird-watching had been something he and Cory had done for hours at a time, hoping to pass the long summer days of their childhood. Today, he found a moment's peace in watching the big bird roam freely through the sky. He watched until it flew out of sight.

The contentment he felt was short-lived, and he was forced back to reality when he thought about the twist fate had dealt him. Who would have thought that the only girl he'd ever loved would have ended up the wife of his brother? And who would have thought he would still care for her after all she'd done to him? But he did. God help him, but he still loved her.

Not that he hadn't tried to find someone else. He'd been involved with several other women over the years. But each time, he'd hoped for the same feeling he'd felt with Lainie, and much to his disappointment, he'd never come close to finding it. After a while he'd finally given up and begun putting his feelings into the words of his songs, and today he was wealthy because of that. But money wasn't everything. He was living proof.

Glancing down at his canvas shoes, he noticed the morning dampness clinging to them.

He'd gotten up early after having lain awake most of the night doing just what he was doing now—gazing around him and thinking, but mostly thinking. His old bedroom felt strange to him, not really much different from the hotel rooms that had become so much a part of his life. Somehow that saddened him. Maybe because he had hoped he would just come home and immediately find the peace that, for so long, had eluded him.

If only he'd been able to talk to Cory while his brother was still fully conscious, before he'd been given large doses of morphine to ease his pain. Then maybe Cory would have understood his motive for staying away. At least they could have come to terms with each other. Maybe, with his brother's help, he could even have forgiven Lainie. But now it was too late. It didn't matter that he loved her. He wanted revenge. He'd often heard there was a thin line between love and hate. Well, Lainie had shoved him over that line at least twice—and that was one time too many.

So where did that leave him emotionally? Why did he feel like a low-down rat for what he planned to do to her? And why did he continue to imagine the two of them making love instead of war?

Maybe he should be thanking her, he thought sarcastically, wanting to feed the sluggish anger within him. After all, it was she who had taught him a hard lesson about women that he would never forget.

He gazed around the backyard of his parents' home. The lush green lawn extended to the narrow bayou two hundred yards away. Shrubs towered over the picket fence bordering his family's property. Climbing roses bloomed in profusion between the slats and over the top of the scalloped edges. Daylilies lined the bottom of the fence, while giant live oak trees stood, blanketed in Spanish moss, spreading their shade across the patio. Being back home felt odd to him right now, but he had a feeling that, given enough time, it could become all too familiar again. He made a mental note not to give himself that much time.

The big collie he'd seen yesterday appeared at his feet, pawing at his leg. Using the moment to his advantage, he bent down and patted the animal's head. "Hey, boy. You're a handsome thing. What's your name, huh?" Zac asked, picking up a small branch and tossing it toward the bayou. "Get it, boy!"

The big shaggy dog flounced off in pursuit.

"Morris."

The sound of Lainie's voice startled Zac. "What?"

"His name's Morris."

"Morris? What kind of a name is that?" he asked, his expression almost comical. Glancing back at the dog, he broke into an earthy grin as he watched the animal retrieve the stick and return it to his feet.

"Alyse named him after Morris, the cat from that commercial. Remember him?"

"Yeah," he answered. "I remember."

What would his daughter say when she learned the truth behind his visit? Would she hate him, or Lainie—or both of them? That was the scary part, the reality, that he had to face sooner or later. She was an innocent lamb in all this, and he didn't want her hurt. Still, he felt it was past time for her to learn who her father really was. Not that he wanted to wipe the memory of his brother from her mind. He just wanted her to find a place in her heart for him, too. He deserved that much, didn't he?

He watched Lainie from a distance as she bent down and pulled a long weed from the rose bed. At the moment, she looked like an innocent, too, as the sun played along the strands of her light brown hair, giving it a healthy glow. She brushed back a lock flying in the breeze and tucked it behind her ear. For a time she seemed to have forgotten he was standing there, and for a time he allowed himself to forget why he'd come back. His thoughts drifted to another era, when their hearts had been on fire and their bodies had yearned to become one.

Lainie, sweet, lovely, Lainie.

A regretful smile tugged at his lips. Why had she lied to him? That was the thought that nagged him at the oddest times. Why? Hadn't she known how much he'd loved her?

"How about a cup of coffee? It should be ready by now," Lainie said, breaking the quiet around them. "I plugged in the coffee maker before coming out."

He threw the branch once more for Morris to retrieve, then fell into step behind her.

He watched as she moved across the yard, as sultry and light as a late-afternoon breeze. He allowed himself the luxury of dwelling on the blue silk robe that clung to her body and made the way she walked seem like such a provocative means of travel.

He'd often thought about a morning like this, just him and Lainie lazily sipping coffee while strolling in the early-morning coolness.

"I saw Alyse last week."

"Alyse!" Lainie exclaimed, whirling around to face him. "Where did you see her?"

"I sent her tickets for last week's performance in the Astrodome," Zachary answered.

"She never mentioned it to me."

"It wasn't that big a deal. I sent her five front-row tickets, and she brought her friends with her. Anyway, isn't she a bit old to be checking out her plans with you? She's nineteen and lives on her own," he said.

"I know how old my daughter is. I don't need you to tell me. And to set the record straight, she's only living in Houston while she's in school. Her home is still here with me."

Lainie walked on to the house and let the back door slam shut behind her. By the time Zachary entered the kitchen, she was plopping four pieces of wheat bread into the toaster, her abrupt movements warning him that she was upset.

From old habit, he went to a cabinet and opened the door, exposing the coffee mugs. His mother's everyday cups had always been there, and it wasn't until he saw the odd, steady glance Lainie gave him that the coincidence registered.

"Mama always kept her cups here. I just didn't think. I'm sorry." He held two white ceramic mugs in his grip, but he set them down like they were hot. "Guess I shouldn't have helped myself."

"Don't be ridiculous," she said, trying to open a new jar of blackberry preserves. "If you're going to..." She stopped speaking as she strained to loosen the top. It finally twisted off. "If you're going to stay here, you'll have to make yourself at home. I don't want to have to worry about you. I have several projects I'm planning to start, and you'll be left to fend for yourself." She set the jar on the table.

Zachary felt the hidden sting of her words. There wasn't any doubt in his mind that she didn't like having him here, and she certainly didn't intend to make it easy for him. Well, the Lainie he remembered would never have backed away from a good fight. Apparently she hadn't changed as much as she would like him to believe.

He poured the coffee, then added sugar and cream. Smiling, he placed a mug near her, pleased with himself for remembering just how she liked it.

"Here you go. Two sugars and one cream."

Lainie glanced sideways at the mug. "I drank it like that years ago. I drink it black now."

"Well, excuse me, Mrs. Benjamin. I should have known better. You keep reminding me of how you've changed. I wonder if you still kiss the same."

The minute the words left his mouth, he knew he'd said the wrong thing. Her face drained of color. Blast! He'd lost his cool, and now she would retreat further from him because of it. Any progress he'd made since arriving was going down the old drainpipe. "I'm sorry, Lainie. I shouldn't have said that."

"You're damn right you shouldn't have said that. First you tell me you've seen Alyse behind my back, and now this. Just how did you know where to find her, anyway?''

"Look, it wasn't like you think. I knew she was in school in Houston, and I just thought it would be a nice thing to do for her since I would be there. You're blowing this all out of proportion. Would you just listen to me—"

"No, I'm not going to listen to you. If you've come here thinking the poor widow will welcome your advances, you're mistaken. Since Cory's death I've had plenty of offers from some of our so-called family friends. I didn't need their sleazy offers of comfort, and I sure as hell don't need yours.''

A sudden jealousy erupted somewhere inside him and ripped through Zac's gut, almost throwing him off balance. But he managed to place his coffee mug on the table before getting up from his chair, his eyes narrowed slits of fire. "Who asked you to go to bed with them?''

Lainie stared into his face, seemingly dumbfounded by his reaction. Finally, after several seconds, her eyes shifted to the toaster. "Oh my God, the bread's stuck again!" she wailed, reaching for the smoking appliance.

"Ooouch!" she yelled, jerking her hand away from the hot metal as the sound of her voice bounced off the kitchen walls.

Before she made another move, Zachary sprang into action. "You've burned yourself," he said, grabbing her wrist and thrusting her fingers under the faucet, turning on the cold water in the process.

"It's nothing," Lainie replied, trying to pull her hand from his. But he held on.

"It'll blister," he said. "You've burned the tips pretty bad. An ice pack would help." He examined the delicate skin on her palm, then the reddened flesh of her finger-tips. "I'll make you one."

"I don't have time, Zachary," she insisted, this time succeeding in freeing her hand. "I need to get ready for school. I'll be late as it is. My fingers are fine, really they are." She turned, bolted out of the kitchen and ran up the stairs.

"Blast," Zachary said under his breath. He followed her to the foot of the staircase and watched as she disappeared. He hated himself for making that stupid remark. She was retreating from him like a frightened little bird, and his task was becoming harder to accomplish by the minute. So why was he more worried about her feelings than he was about his plan?

Watch it, Benjamin, his inner voice warned. She's really getting to you. Cursing himself for an idiot, he turned back to the kitchen.

Later during the morning, just before he went outside to mow the lawn, the phone rang. It was Bobby Jones, his manager.

"Zachary, where the devil are you?" Jones asked the moment Zac picked up the receiver. "I had to get this number from your answering service. Took me some fancy talkin', too. What's gotten into you? Come on back here to Nashville, son. We got that big benefit for abused children coming up. I need you here."

"I need a rest, Bobby."

"Son, you're not listenin' to me," Bobby said. "We need you here today—right now."

"Well, that's just too bad. I need some time to my-self."

"You're not doing something stupid, are you? Like marrying one of those little gals that hang around the re-cording studio mooning after you? You haven't gotten some woman pregnant, have you? Good Lord, it'll be front page news before we know it. You'll be ruined.''

"Come off it, Bobby. I thought you knew me better than that. I'm not into that kind of stuff, and you know it.''

"Okay, okay,'' Bobby said, laughing nervously. "But you had me worried for a minute there.''

"Look, we've been together for a long time. You know me as well as anyone. So when I tell you not to worry about anything, you should know I've got everything under control. I need a little time to myself, that's all. I'll be back in plenty of time for the benefit. You can count on it.''

"It's just you've never done anything like this before.''

"Don't you think I was due for a vacation after twenty years?''

"Sure, son, sure. Just don't be so mysterious next time. It makes me nervous.''

"I'll keep in touch. Oh—and, Bobby, don't call me again unless it's an emergency, like the earth opened up and swallowed up Tennessee. Got it?''

"See what I mean. You ain't used to acting like—''

Zachary hung up the receiver.

He spent the remainder of the morning mowing the lawn, taking off his shirt and enjoying south Louisiana's early-summer sun on his back. It had been a long time since he'd perspired from working in the heat, and it felt good.

When he finished, he went upstairs to shower and was confronted by a black pair of Lainie's hose that she had hung up to dry on the shower rod. His heart pounded as he rubbed the silky nylons between his fingers. Licking his dry lips, he pulled them from the rod and slid them down the side of his face. They felt soft against the stubble of his day-old beard. Whatever she had washed them in smelled sweet and delicious and made him think of her walking toward him in a meadow of wildflowers wearing only panties and a bra and a black garter belt holding up the nylons he had in his hand.

His imagination was going wild.

So was his body.

He could almost feel her body beneath his, causing a raging heat to rise in his loins.

Suddenly he thrust the nylons aside as if they were hot. And in a way they were, because he was on fire.

When he stepped out of the shower ten minutes later, the only sound he could hear was the constant humming of the air conditioner. It was a lonely sound.

With a towel wrapped around his waist, he stood in the doorway that led to Lainie's room and gazed around. For a moment he almost let himself feel sorry for her. After all, she was all alone in this big old house, with only the walls of her bedroom to hold her at night. Did they whisper sweet words of comfort to her the way a lover would? Did she tell them her needs, her desires, her dreams? Did she ever think of him?

He put an abrupt halt to his thoughts when he saw where they were leading and stormed into his own room to dress.

As he headed downstairs, he spotted her wedding picture in the upstairs hallway. He'd noticed it before, but he'd forced himself to walk by without looking closely. But this time was different. This time he stopped.

Cory and Lainie stared back at him, smiles on both their faces. Cory looked the same as always, but Lainie's eyes tugged at some hidden emotion deep inside him. There was a glimmer in their depths. Something he couldn't really define. Was it disappointment? Sadness? No, it couldn't be. He had to be wrong. This had been her wedding day, the day she'd so deviously planned all along. Why should she have been anything but happy?

How could I have been such a fool for her?

Hoping to clear his head, he headed back outside.

Lainie entered the house and dropped her purse on a nearby chair. She'd suffered all she could of Debra Cohen's chatter about her houseguest and now she had a headache.

According to Debra, Zachary Benjamin was the hottest thing since Rhett Butler. The woman had not shut up for one single minute the entire day.

And then to announce she was throwing a party tonight in his honor, an honor he had gladly accepted when Debra phoned him during afternoon break . . . !

Debra's exact quote of his answer had been, "Great. Lainie and I would love to come."

Like hell she would. She didn't want to go anywhere with him. She didn't even want him in her house—his house—oh, what the heck, she thought, frustrated with herself and everything around her. If the remaining days of his visit were going to be anything like yesterday and this morning, she was thinking about getting herself a room at the motel fifteen miles up the road.

It was going as badly as she had expected. Everywhere she turned, his presence was there. An empty beer can on the counter. A sweaty T-shirt tossed over the back of a chair. There wasn't a single moment during the day when he wasn't on her mind. She didn't need this kind of mental harassment.

And all because he'd had a sudden whim to return home for a few days. For twenty years he hadn't bothered to set foot inside his family home. Now, all of a sudden, he needed a rest. Big deal!

"Hi."

Lainie whirled around and was confronted by the subject of her thoughts.

She tried to ignore the fluttering of her heart at the sight meeting her eyes. Wearing a white shirt unbuttoned to the waist, Zachary leaned casually against the wall, an earthshaking grin on his face as he stood there, drinking a beer. His dark hair hung across his forehead in a way that would have rattled any red-blooded woman. Lainie told herself the sensation traveling through her body was nothing more than a misplaced feeling of regret at knowing what could have been.

"You're the typical schoolteacher with your hair up in that bun and your glasses perched on your nose," he said, reaching out and removing them from her face. She reached up to stop him, but she was too late.

"Be careful or you'll break them," she said anxiously.

Ignoring her remark, he pushed himself away from the wall and laid her glasses on the counter. "Do you know you still remind me of the young girl I held in my arms at the movies and fed popcorn to, one kernel at a time? Do you remember that?" He reached for her face.

She slapped his hand away. "That was a long time ago, Zac," she said, attempting to walk past him, but failing when he blocked her way with that gorgeous body of his. His nonchalant behavior pricked her temper. "I don't even eat popcorn very often anymore."

She looked at him in a way that made it clear she wanted him to move so she could get by, but he didn't budge. "It isn't the popcorn I'm talking about, Lainie, and you know it. It was the mood, the way we were."

It infuriated her that her insides cried out in bitter-sweet anguish every time she remembered those days. And she hated the way she still felt hot all over when he looked at her with those penetrating green eyes of his, as if he were suffering, too. "I said I don't remember," she ground out.

"And I can't seem to forget. The memories are branded on my mind.... The way you felt when I held you in my arms.... The way our mouths melted together when we kissed.... All the delicious little things we used to do to each other. I can't believe you don't remember them, too."

She remembered, all right. All too well. Night after night, year after year, she'd felt guilty because she remembered all too well. Because there was Cory, lying beside her, loving her when he knew she still loved his brother in a way she could never love him. It wasn't fair. Dear God, none of it was fair.

Suddenly she found herself backed against the wall.

"You loved me back then, with every inch of your body. You worked your way into my dreams. You even promised to love me forever, Lainie."

She could hardly breathe. Someone had placed a vise around her throat and was tightening it with each passing second. This whole thing was getting out of hand. Just who did he think he was? He had no right to use that accusing tone of voice with her. He was acting as if the last twenty years were all her fault. "I had nothing to do with your dreams—and I can't see where you've suffered any."

"Then maybe you'd better look closer," he said, pushing her against the wall with his body. His emerald eyes scorched her face like a flame as he pressed himself against her. "If you can't see it, then maybe you can feel it."

His hand wrapped around her neck and forced her face within inches of his, his breath warm and moist and smelling vaguely of alcohol. "Can you feel it now?" he asked as his mouth opened against her cheek.

She felt his lips and tongue tasting her flesh. She went hot all over. Her knees almost buckled.

"Yes," she answered breathlessly. "Oh . . . yes. . . ."

With that, his mouth crushed down on hers, hot and demanding, unleashing feelings Lainie would have sold her soul to deny. But they were there, in the way her fingers gripped his waist and pulled him closer, in the way she responded to the ferocity of his kiss.

A hot flame of desire engulfed her. She held on to him, knowing full well that her body was too shaken by the hard feel of him pressed against her to stand on its own.

Slowly the kiss became less demanding, more tender, teasing the sensitivity of her mouth and making her moan with a need to have him in the way she'd been denied for twenty years.

"Sweet, lovely Lainie," he murmured against her mouth. "I've been wanting to have you like this for so long, it seems impossible my wish has finally been granted."

For several long seconds they clung together, neither speaking. Then, as if a cold glass of water had suddenly doused her face, Lainie jerked away. She was damp with perspiration. So was he.

Zachary let her go and ran his fingers through his already disheveled hair.

"Well," he said, his voice still husky with desire, "I think your memory is every bit as good as mine." His grin became cocky. "At least we can call ourselves friends again."

No longer cornered, Lainie turned and practically ran for the stairs. After taking several steps up, she stopped and faced him. "We were never friends, Zachary. Cory and I were friends. But you never needed anyone but yourself."

"Is that a fact?" he asked, meeting her gaze with sarcasm. "Well, just how would you know? You were so self-centered I don't think you gave one thought to my feelings."

Lainie stared at him with visible contempt. "Coming from the likes of you, I'll ignore that insult." She turned around and stormed the rest of the way up the stairs.

"Too chicken to stay and fight?" he asked. "I should have known."

When she reached the top, she faced him again. "No— I'm the one who should've known. There's only one reason why you've come back, and that's to antagonize me."

"I'm not that kind of guy."

"You most certainly are."

If her remark hurt his feelings in any way, he recovered from it with a quick grin that inched its way across his face. "I've been told a lot worse."

She clenched her teeth. "I just bet you have." She wanted to scream at him, but instead she headed for her bedroom. Her head pounded. So did her heart. She was a fool to let him get to her like this.

She had thought that would be the last of him for a while, but just as she walked into her bedroom, she heard him say, "Be sure and dress real pretty for the party tonight. Will you be wearing the black stockings hanging in the bath?"

In answer, she slammed the door to her room.

Black stockings? Oh, for crying out loud, she thought suddenly. She'd probably left them drying on the shower rod, the way she always did.

Her head throbbed even more. She undressed and slipped into her robe, then tried lying across her bed, but that didn't help. She could hear Zachary roaming around next door. Surely he wasn't already getting ready for tonight's party. It was still hours away.

Well, at least her headache was a perfect excuse for not attending Debra's little get-together. She certainly didn't want to go.

From what her friend had said, it would be like a reunion. Although Debra was younger by a few years and hadn't been a part of the gang that had hung around with Zac back in high school, she'd deliberately invited as many of those classmates as she could find on such short notice. And according to her, they were all coming—*with plenty of memories of the good old days*.

Lainie stood, tightened her robe around her body and tied the sash. Then she walked to the dresser and ran an unconscious finger along the frame of the family photograph that seemed to catch her eye so often these days.

Cory. Her sweet, sincere Cory. Would she ever forgive herself for not being able to offer him the same kind of love he'd given to her?

His twinkling eyes smiled at her just as she remembered him doing so many times. And she couldn't help herself. Sadly, she smiled back. He'd said she'd made him a very happy man, but since his death, there were times when she wondered. Had she really?

She shifted her gaze to Zachary. She tried not to think about the kiss moments ago. Good Lord, if she did, she'd go crazy. And if nothing else, her pride refused to allow that to happen. Besides, she owed Cory. Maybe she hadn't felt for him the same way he had felt for her, but she *had* loved him, and she could make sure his memory was given the respect it deserved.

Hearing a soft knock at her door, she walked to answer it, thinking how life was often unfair.

"Coming," she answered when the knock became more urgent. She yanked open the door. "What...?" The rest of her question evaporated like a child's warm breath on a frosty morning.

Zachary stood there, a towel wrapped around his waist, the flaps not quite meeting at the bottom, leaving an eight-inch slit that invited her shocked gaze.

Lainie's breath locked in her throat, smothering out all ability to speak. Thank goodness the opening was located along his side and not down the front of his perfect, masculine body.

Not that she thought it would have bothered him any to be standing there before her in his full naked glory— and not that she would have looked if he had.

Slowly her gaze slid up his torso, passing his navel, partially hidden in tangled hair, traveling higher as the dark curly hair spread out to cover his lean muscled chest.

Lainie swallowed, her gaze meeting his. The impact of it was like having physical contact with a devil.

"I, uh, need soap," he said, grinning.

"Soap," Lainie repeated stupidly, as a sudsy, lazy sensation slid through her.

"Yeah," he answered, sounding to her as lazy as the sensation cruising through her body. "The stuff that washes away your cares and lets you feel comfortable in a crowd." His grin had broadened.

"Uh, there's soap in the cabinet under the sink. Just look—"

"I did," he replied, his eyes daring and mischievous. "I looked everywhere."

Lainie brushed him aside, then trotted across the hall. Zac followed close behind. As soon as she reached the bathroom, she dropped to one knee and swung open the cabinet door beneath the sink, then began rummaging through the small but cluttered compartment.

"Here," she said. She was totally exasperated with him and didn't bother to look in his direction. She had had about all she could handle of Zachary Benjamin clothed in a designer towel.

"You'd better shower as soon as I finish or we'll be late for the party," he said.

With her eyes still staring at the plumbing beneath the sink, she ground out, "Thank you just the same, but I think I'll know when it's time for me to shower."

"I was just making sure you weren't trying to cop out on our date for the party."

"It's not a date, for heaven's sake."

"Well, whatever it is, we're going together."

If the towel wrapped around his waist had been a magic carpet descending from the sky as it fell to the floor beside her, Lainie couldn't have been more shocked. Feeling her insides turn soft and trembly, she clung to the cabinet for support. All she had to do was turn her head and she would be eye level with his... Oh, good Lord, she was really going off the deep end.

When the shower door closed seconds later, she thanked heaven for the small favor, scrambled to her feet and flew out of the bathroom just as Zachary began singing in a loud, clear voice.

Chapter Four

Two hours later Lainie walked out of her bedroom, running her fingers through her hair, hoping to fluff out the freshly shampooed strands. After having fought with it for an hour, she'd decided to pull it up on one side of her head with a tortoiseshell comb, and to heck with what anyone thought of her hairdo. For heaven's sake, it was just another one of Debra's parties. The woman had them all the time. The fact that the guest of honor was Zachary Benjamin didn't make it any more of a big deal.

She'd deliberately chosen a soft pink gauze dress with a scooped neckline and straps that tied on top of each shoulder. She always got plenty of compliments when she wore it. The leather sandals she'd slipped on her feet had crisscrossing straps of different pastel colors, and small seashells dangling from her ears completed her summer look.

She started down the stairs, certain Zachary was irritated with her for being late. Well, she was irritated, too.

Whoever heard of a guest walking around in a bath towel? It wasn't as if they were married! They weren't even kin. Not really. Certainly no decent person in Harrington would ever do such a thing. Most certainly not herself.

As she descended the staircase, she saw him lounging in a chair, a beer bottle in one hand. He lifted it to his lips and took a deep swallow. Lainie watched as his Adam's apple bobbed up and down.

She could never deny his handsomeness, not even to herself. Like tonight. Sitting there in his dove-gray dinner jacket that molded itself to his wide shoulders, he looked every bit as good as he did in the starched and ironed pin-striped shirts and blue jeans that were so much a part of his image. But then, she reminded herself, she had never denied his dark good looks. It was his character she had learned to doubt.

He'd combed his hair back, and it was in place about as well as it was ever going to be. Lainie knew he'd long ago lost the battle with an uncontrollable wave that gave the dark, shiny mane a life of its own. She remembered carelessly running her fingers through its coarse texture. He'd worn it longer then, and she'd enjoyed messing it up—which, she recalled, usually resulted in an argument between them. But they'd always made up in the end, which was probably why they argued in the first place.

Oh, God, just for tonight, let me forget all those times, she pleaded.

Zachary saw her and stood, but other than a slight gleam in his deep green eyes, his expression didn't change as she approached.

Lainie's stomach did a somersault. She felt like a young girl coming downstairs for her first date. Unconsciously, she ran her tongue along her lips before smiling.

"You look beautiful in pink," he said. "Your complexion glows. It's definitely your best color. And your hair looks great like that. It's sexy pulled back on one side," he said, grinning. "Did you wear the black hose?" he asked, bending down to get a look at her legs.

"No, I did not," Lainie said, her smile faltering as she took a step back.

"Too bad."

"You really have some nerve, Zachary."

"And you don't have enough. What happened to you over the years? You used to be so much fun."

"I bet I was. Fun and easy."

She could see that her words shocked him. Well, they shocked her, too. She couldn't believe she'd said that.

But hadn't she been thinking of herself in that way for years now?

His eyes narrowed. "It wasn't like that, and you know it."

She couldn't think straight and stood gaping at him as tears gathered in her eyes.

Zachary reached for her, his face a mass of conflicting emotions. "Lainie..."

She heard a note of pity in his voice—pity, of all things—and it caused her dignity to suffer its worst blow ever.

And yet when he pulled her into his arms, she let him. She needed him to comfort her. She needed him, and only him, to wipe away the pain of the moment. But would he want to?

She buried herself in his embrace, wrapping her arms around his waist and breathing in his strength, the very strength she would have to use soon to pull away.

He groaned and crushed her body to his, his hands running wildly over her back. "Oh, Lainie. You were never that way."

His body was hard and hot and all man—and she was tired of fighting a losing battle. She wanted to hear his lying words of love—even if he'd spoken them to a hundred different women over the last twenty years. She wanted them and needed them now, in this moment, more than she needed oxygen to breathe.

She was soft and warm and all woman in his arms, and he was tired of fighting a losing battle. Suddenly he wanted more than revenge. He wanted her—period. And she wanted him, too. He was sure of it.

His lips trailed along her temple, slowly traveling downward to her pliant lips. In the next second his mouth covered hers with a need so overpowering that neither of them could pull away.

The kiss was hot, urgent and totally sensual. Twenty years of anger and hate and love and simple human need came together in brazen fury.

Locked into a timeless moment, neither heard the telephone ringing the first time. But when it stopped and then started again, it shattered the moment. Lainie shoved him away as if she'd just awakened from a dream. Shaking from head to toe, she bit her bottom lip to stop its trembling and reached for the receiver. She hesitated long enough to draw a deep breath before speaking. Still, her greeting sounded strange.

"Lainie? Is that you?" Debra asked, though she continued talking without waiting for a reply. "When are the two of you going to get here? Everybody's just standing around waiting."

Lainie took another shaky breath. "We're leaving now," she said, pressing her fingers to her throbbing lips. "We should be there in a few minutes."

"Good. A party isn't much fun without the guest of honor. Tell Zachary we're waiting for him."

After a quick goodbye, Lainie hung up. "That was Debra. She says everyone is waiting for you to arrive."

There, she thought. She'd sounded normal. Now, if she could just face him without batting an eyelash, she'd have it made.

Zac waited for her to turn in his direction. Those few precious moments when she had come willingly into his arms had been like having a taste of heaven after being in hell for twenty long endless years.

That kiss had just happened. It wasn't something he'd planned. Recognizing a need in her, he'd acted on pure instinct.

He was playing with fire, and he knew it.

He'd almost lost control, and that scared him. There was only one reason for his being here, and it had nothing to do with letting things between him and Lainie *just happen*.

Lainie straightened her shoulders. "Don't you ever do that again. If you do, I'll make you leave this house," she said, sounding as if she were in total control. Her only giveaway was the fact that she still didn't face him.

"I think you're forgetting something. This happens to be *my* house."

Her shoulders stiffened. "Then I'll be the one leaving."

He shrugged. "Suit yourself. But where would you go?"

She whirled around. "I'll find a place," she said furiously.

"Go ahead," he said, folding his arms and loving every minute of her discomfort. His mouth lifted at the corners.

Her eyes blazed. "You think I can't, is that it?"

He laughed out loud. "Beggars can't be choosers. Maybe I'll let you stay."

Her insides seethed with anger. "That does it. I'm leaving." She marched toward the stairs.

He grabbed her by the upper arm. "Oh, no, you're not."

"You can't stop me."

"I bet I can." He grinned wickedly. "If you walk out this door, I'll go to that party alone and tell everybody there that you moved out because you had the hots for me so bad you couldn't control yourself."

Her brown eyes widened in horror. "You wouldn't dare," she finally managed to say.

His grin spread across his face. "Try me."

"I hate you."

"Now we're getting somewhere."

"I don't care what you tell everyone. Let go of me."

"Sure," he said, dropping her arm. She started for the door. "Lainie, if you leave, I swear I'll sell this house and all your precious memories with it."

She froze. Then, after a few moments, she slowly turned to face him. "That's blackmail."

He smirked. "Yeah, I guess it is."

"You're despicable."

"You've already made that quite clear." He glanced at his wristwatch. "I'm leaving for the party in exactly three minutes. What happens to this place is up to you." With that, he walked out the door.

How could she have ever thought she loved him? Lainie wondered, the slamming of the door echoing in her mind.

Zachary walked to the car, shaken to the bone. Lainie had a way of getting to him. Like his saying he would sell the old house. He could never do something like that. But he'd never tell her differently. Not now that he knew he could use that threat to control her.

Benjamin, you're back in the driver's seat, he told himself.

So why didn't he feel like gloating?

He sat behind the wheel and looked at his watch. His heart began to pound as his deadline drew nearer and Lainie still didn't come out of the house. As realization poured over him like a midsummer rain, he felt a moment of panic. Damn her, she was going to call his bluff. Now what?

He cranked the engine, threw the gears in reverse and accelerated the engine. The Jag flew back about ten feet before he braked, scattering gravel. He shifted into drive and gunned the motor, sending the car zooming to the front of the house. Just about the time he hit the horn, Lainie came flying out the door.

See, Benjamin, he told himself. You *are* in control.

Unconsciously, he released the breath he'd been holding.

They drove to the party in silence. Lainie brooded in her seat, while Zachary careened around one curve after another. His heart was still pounding like crazy. What would he have done if she hadn't come out when she had? Thank God he didn't have to come up with an answer to that one.

Debra met them at the door. Zac gave her a kiss on the cheek and presented her with the bottle of champagne he'd bought earlier in the day. It wasn't his usual brand, but it was all he could find in the one supermarket in Harrington. "For our lovely hostess."

Debra practically swooned.

Their arrival was met with a maelstrom of activity. Of course, just as Lainie had suspected, Zachary was the center of attention for every guest, male and female alike.

They finally made their way through the crowd waiting just beyond the doorway. Debra led them to the bar and offered them a drink. Zac mixed himself a Scotch and water, then made Lainie a Fuzzy Navel after a friend suggested the cocktail and Lainie decided to try it. She politely accepted the drink when he handed it to her. It was all an act, but she felt it was necessary in order to keep the busy tongues of her friends from wagging about them. This little town was no different from most others across the country. Everyone here loved a juicy story, and if any ingredient was missing from the plot, they usually spiced things up by simply adding to it. She didn't need that. Zachary had added all the cayenne pepper to her life her stomach could handle.

As the night wore on, Zachary remained the center of attention. Every female in the place turned her charm on him full force. It was so obvious it was sickening. Lainie watched as they sashayed up to him and, even though their husbands were standing right there, flirted with him like a bunch of hussies.

Not that he appeared to mind. As a matter of fact, he seemed to be having a great time. Though he returned to her side often during the next couple of hours, he was always swept away again by one guest after another. And, like the perfect gentleman he was, he was attentive to each of them.

Lainie sipped the glass of wine she'd chosen when her peach-flavored concoction was gone, chatted pleasantly and tried to act as though he were no different than anyone else in attendance. When anyone asked a question about him, she made certain she referred to him as her brother-in-law when she answered. She even managed to smile a couple of times. But no matter how much she attempted to keep her eyes from drifting to where he was, time after time she found herself almost staring in his direction. She felt something akin to jealousy when she noticed her friends batting their eyelashes at him. But what really bothered her was that he seemed to enjoy it so much. She felt like slapping that cockeyed grin clean off his face.

And he thought he could control her. Well, she wasn't ready to surrender just yet. Maybe she *had* flown out of the house when she thought he was leaving, but hadn't he waited past his three-minute ultimatum?

She heard a flirtatious giggle and saw a redhead whom she didn't recognize whispering something in his ear. Zachary noticed Lainie looking at him and gave her a wink over the other woman's shoulder just as the redhead pulled away. Lainie turned and walked across the room. She made herself join a small group of friends who were discussing Louisiana politics, an always colorful topic of conversation. She felt she had to do something to occupy her thoughts so they didn't keep creeping back to *him*.

At odd times he seemed equally aware of what she was doing or with whom she spoke. Often their gazes would lock for several seconds, and he would give her a grin or a wink.

"Attentive, isn't he? Is the flame of years ago rekindling itself?" Debra Cohen asked near Lainie's ear.

"No—of course not. That was a long time ago. We were just kids."

"Well, the two of you certainly aren't kids anymore."

Lainie looked at her friend. Debra had an exuberant personality and spoke of her life and past lovers the same way she did everything else, with little regard to what people thought. "What is that supposed to mean?"

"Nothing. I was just stating a fact. Boy, I bet he's really something in bed. Wouldn't you just love to find out for yourself?"

"No, as a matter of fact, I would not."

"Oh, come off it, Lainie. Don't tell me you're sharing the same house with him and don't fantasize about such things. Are you blind?"

"No, just smart. I'm not interested in a fling—and I imagine that's all a woman would ever get from him."

Debra's eyebrows rose. "Are you speaking from experience?"

Lainie turned furious eyes to her friend. "My relationship with Zachary was nothing like that."

"Whatever you say, honey," Debra stated, gazing around the room. In the next breath she added, "But that's not how I remember it."

"I can't believe you, Debra. Maybe you should read my lips very carefully. There's nothing between Zachary and me."

"Uh-huh," Debra said, as though humoring her. Then, in the next breath, she added, "Would you look over there? Dan has just spilled his third drink on my new rug. I gotta go. We'll talk about it later."

"There's nothing more to talk about," Lainie said to her friend's retreating back. Why didn't Debra believe her? Why didn't she believe herself?

She hadn't had the time to figure out the answer before the redheaded woman who had been leaning all over Zac waltzed up to her.

"Honey, if he's half as good as he looks, I envy you."

"I beg your pardon."

"I envy you," she said, nudging Lainie's side. "Tell me, does he love as good as he looks?" The woman smiled at Lainie as if she already knew the answer.

"That's none of your business," Lainie said, pivoting on her heel and strutting off. Now why had she said that? Wasn't it as good as admitting *she* knew the answer, too?

Zachary appeared out of nowhere, grabbed her by the arm and eased her to his side. "What's wrong?"

"Nothing."

"Nothing? Come on, Lainie, what's wrong? Did that woman say something to upset you?"

Lainie drew a deep breath. "The whole town seems to think we're—we're sleeping together," she stammered.

Zac hiked up one eyebrow. "Now that's not a bad idea."

"You would think that," she said with a sneer.

He laughed. "Look, it's just idle gossip. Don't pay it any mind."

Lainie looked at him as if she thought he'd gone mad. "And when you're gone, I'll be the one living here, right in the middle of it."

He leaned closer, a devilish grin on his face. "Then maybe we shouldn't let it just be gossip. If you're going to live with the stigma anyway.... Why don't we live up to their wildest expectations?" His green eyes sparkled like gems. "So what will it be, your bed or mine?"

Lainie narrowed her eyes. "You're drunk," she ground out, taking a step away from him.

He made a grab for her waist. "No, I'm not. Just feeling good enough to say I'd like nothing better than to make mad, passionate love to you tonight."

Anger bubbled up inside her. "So now the truth's out. You've come home thinking you can charm me into your bed. This is all a game to you, isn't it? That's what this whole thing is all about," she said, allowing her anger and frustration to get the better of her. "You're hateful," she said, much louder than she'd intended. Then, turning, she stalked from the room.

"Lainie," Zac called after her. She didn't stop. "Well, you can run all you want, but you can't run away forever." Then, under his breath, he added, "And I'll be here forever, if that's what it takes."

Everyone in the room stopped speaking. Some wore expressions of surprise, while others smiled, as if to say they'd always known there were still some strong feelings between those two.

Lainie flounced across the room without a backward glance and marched through the door without stopping for her purse. She wanted to go home. To hell with Zachary and the townspeople and anyone else who wanted to pry into her life. It was *her* life, not theirs.

The hot, sultry night slapped her in the face as she headed for the car, though she was now sane enough to realize she wasn't going anywhere. It was Zachary's car, and he had the keys.

She was so frustrated and angry—and hurt—that she felt like crying. She didn't hear the sound of footsteps approaching, but a half second later she sensed someone behind her just before sinewy arms encircled her waist and held her immobile.

"Let me go!" she exclaimed.

"Who are you running from, Lainie? Me, or yourself?"

"Let go of me, Zachary. You have no right—"

"I have every right," he said, pulling her flat against his body. "Now—please—stop fighting me."

"Let me go," she said, near tears.

"Okay, as soon as you calm down." He held her until she stopped struggling. "Now, wait here while I get your things and make an excuse to Debra. For someone who said she didn't want to cause a commotion that would have the whole town talking, you sure gave them something that will keep them busy for the next ten years. I think everyone's watching us."

Oh, wonderful, Lainie's mind screamed. Of all the foolish, idiotic things for her to do. Disgusted with the entire night, she leaned against him and stared up at the sky. "Remember when we used to count the stars?" She gave a pained sigh. "We could never count them all, could we?"

Zac's breath quickened. Damn her, she was doing it to him again. He was falling under her spell. Abruptly pulling away, he said, "Wait here."

By the time he returned, she'd calmed down, though her pride was suffering something awful.

He didn't have to tell her to get in the car when he unlocked the door. She slipped inside and wished it was a rocket that would take her to the moon.

"I apologized to Debra and said you'd been under a strain, with my return and all. I explained that we'd been reminiscing about the old days, which brought back memories of Cory—"

"And they believed you?" Lainie asked hopefully.

"I don't think so. Not if their expressions meant anything."

"Great," she sighed, staring at the passing countryside.

"It's time for us to do some talking, Lainie. We've been avoiding it long enough."

"Talking? About what?"

"Us."

"What about us?"

"You know perfectly well what about us."

The remaining ride home was silent.

As they pulled into the drive, Zachary chastised himself for a fool. Why was he feeling sorry for her? Lainie was a survivor. She went after what she needed and took it any way she could.

So she was upset. That didn't mean she wasn't capable of taking care of herself without his help. Hadn't she proven that at the tender age of seventeen?

He parked and then went around to open her door. The rustling of their clothing echoed in the darkness as they walked up the path to the house. Zac fumbled with the key in the lock before the door finally swung open. He motioned for Lainie to enter first. She did so without hesitating.

She placed her purse on the Victorian table that had belonged to her grandmother, one of the few traces of her life that she'd brought to this house. Zachary slipped his jacket off and tossed it across the back of the sofa.

"Some night," he said, loosening his tie.

Lainie didn't bother to answer.

"How about a nightcap?" he asked, pouring himself a swallow of whiskey.

"I could use one," she answered quickly. "Just wine, please."

She sat on the sofa. After setting her glass on the table next to her, Zac walked to the mantel and leaned one arm on the edge. Slowly lifting his glass to his lips, he stared into the empty fireplace as though he were watching a roaring fire.

Finally, he spoke. "Let me ask you something. Why do you think I've come home?"

She swung her wide eyes to him. "You said you needed a rest."

He turned his gaze to her, its intensity heating her body several degrees. "Yes, I know what I said. But you don't believe me, do you?"

Moments sifted by without her answering. Without removing his eyes from her, he gulped the rest of his drink. "Well?"

"Not entirely. I—I think there's more, though I can't imagine what it could be," she added quickly. "But this is your house, and you have every right to come here any time you feel like it."

"In a way I *was* homesick," he said quietly, "but my main reason for coming back was so you and I can make peace with each other. After all, except for Alyse, and with both our parents dead, we're the only family either of us has."

Lainie's chest tightened. Had she been wrong about him? "Do you really mean that? Do you really want to be friends?"

"Yes."

"Are you sure there isn't more to it than that?"

Zachary hesitated. "No, of course not."

"And you need a rest?"

Stepping closer to her, he nodded. "Yes."

Her heart picked up tempo. "Well," she said nervously, "I don't know—we're like strangers to each other."

"But we don't have to be. Give us a chance, Lainie."

She stood and placed her empty glass on the table. Avoiding his gaze, she said, "I guess I haven't made things easy for you."

"Hardly!"

"Then I apologize." She turned for the stairs.

"Lainie?"

She spun around at the sound of his voice. "Yes?"

"Do you ever get lonely? Now that you're alone, I mean?"

She bit the corner of her bottom lip. "Sometimes," she said. "But I try not to think about it." She started to turn away again, then stopped and gazed back at him. "Why do you ask?"

"Just wondering. Good night." *Sleep well, my once sweet lover.*

When Lainie reached her bedroom, she undressed and slipped into her gown. Walking to her dresser, she opened a small blue porcelain music box that Zachary had given her on her seventeenth birthday.

He'd been so good-looking back then.... Tall, lean...with a pocket full of dreams. Dreams he'd promised to share with her. But he'd lied. All the promises he'd made were empty, words he'd known she'd wanted to hear. He hadn't loved her. The word *love* came as easily to him as a simple greeting did to most people. He'd played with her the way a child plays with a new toy until it becomes old and used, like all his others. And she would never forgive herself for being the innocent little fool who'd let Zachary Benjamin use her for his amusement until better and more exciting things came his way.

Easy. She had been as easy for him as breathing. With trembling fingers, Lainie closed the box. If she chose to, she could hum its entire melody from memory. If she chose to. But she didn't, not now. Tonight her feelings for him were much too raw. Tears gathered in her eyes. She knew there was no way they could ever be real friends. Too much had happened between them in the past, and because of it there were too many things that could never be said.

A short time later, she cried herself to sleep.

Chapter Five

Zachary stood at the far corner of the garage, his patience worn down to the breadth of a hair. His eyes rested on the source of his frustration.

Lainie.

Her change in attitude toward him since the party two nights ago crippled his every attempt to reach her. Apparently she had decided to put some distance between them—and not just physical distance, but emotional distance, as well.

And she was succeeding.

Oh, she smiled a lot and greeted him pleasantly enough, but her eyes gave her true feelings away.

And he couldn't take much more. He had come here with the intention of breaking her spirit, but from the looks of things, he was the only one suffering.

He had a good mind to just walk over to the swing, yank her off, carry her upstairs and make love to her. The frustrating knowledge that he wanted to do just that—

and not for any reason resembling revenge—wasn't, by any means, helping his black mood.

Just who the devil did she think she was? With one leg hiked up and the other dangling over the side, she appeared totally engrossed in the book she'd carried around with her for the past two days. Undetected, Zachary appraised her long shapely legs, his eyes traveling from her bare feet to the cutoff jeans hugging her skin. His body strained against the hot, wild desire rushing through his loins.

He closed his eyes and found the sweet, honeyed taste of her still coating his memory as though they had made love just yesterday. After a moment, he once again allowed his heated gaze to travel the length of her legs. His mouth dried to the feel of sandpaper. The last time he'd made love to her, they'd been just kids experimenting with newfound feelings. What he wanted now, more than anything, was to make love to the mature woman she'd become.

"I'm thinking like a fool," he said under his breath. Grabbing the toothpick he'd been clenching between his teeth, he flicked it to the ground, spun on his heels and headed for the house, slamming the back door behind him. If he stayed there one more minute, he was going to explode.

He was out the door again in a matter of seconds, stalking toward her. He stopped about ten feet from where she sat reading that darn book of hers, not trusting himself to get any closer. He shoved the camouflage cap he'd plopped on his head farther back, then just stood there with his hands on his hips, staring at her. For some unexplainable reason, he felt his temper rising as he watched her slowly lift her lovely head and turn in his direction.

At first she looked annoyed. As if he were intruding. But then that look evaporated when she met his determined gaze. Zac held on to a moment's triumph when he saw her eyes widen in surprise.

"Are you going somewhere?" she asked, her large, lucid eyes taking in his attire. The paperback novel slipped unnoticed from her hands and fell to the ground.

"Yeah—I thought I'd go into town and meet up with some of the guys who still hang around at Randall's after work. Maybe I can get in a couple of games of pool."

"Oh...well...have a good time," she said. He thought she looked relieved.

"Yeah...well, look...uh...I may be late, so don't bother to fix supper for me."

"Oh, I won't," she said pleasantly. Almost too pleasantly.

Damn, couldn't she at least act like she'd miss his company? "And don't wait up tonight. You know how it is when a bunch of old buddies get together."

"Don't worry. I won't wait up," she said, removing her glasses and gazing at him.

"You'll be all right, won't you?"

"Of course. Why would you ask?"

"Well, it's just the other night you said you get lonely sometimes."

She straightened, and from the look on her face, he could tell he had hit a nerve. His heart leaped.

"I know I said that," she said quickly, irritably. "But everyone gets lonely. It's no big deal."

"Oh, okay," he replied, wanting his answer to be as nonchalant as hers. "Well, fine. Look, I'll see you later."

"Fine. Have fun," she replied, reaching down for her book, wearing the same plastic smile on her face that she'd been giving him all morning.

"Fine, I will," he said, hurrying away before he could jerk her into his arms and demand that she miss him, if only for a moment.

Inhaling deeply, Lainie glanced at the clock on the mantel. She had been looking for her missing watch for over an hour. She knew she was often guilty of removing it unconsciously and placing it on a table or shelf. But thus far, she'd come up empty-handed, and she was beginning to fear she'd never find it.

It was just that she had so many knickknacks lying around, she was probably overlooking it, she told herself. Walking around the parlor, she scanned every tabletop.

Convinced it wasn't anywhere to be found, she went back into the kitchen to have another look, though she'd already covered every inch of that room, too.

She remembered having it on her wrist after lunch because she recalled looking at the time when she'd left the house to go for a walk along the bayou. That had been around three. . . .

She frowned. She had to find that watch. Cory had given it to her on their last anniversary, and the engraving on the back was very special to her.

Deciding the keepsake wasn't in the house, she turned her thoughts to the outside. Could it have fallen off as she'd strolled along Boggy? That thought distressed her. If so, the odds were that she would never find it. But she certainly wasn't going to give up without trying. And she had to do it now—before dark—because if she waited until tomorrow, something as small as a wristwatch would be almost impossible to locate, especially if a thunderstorm came up during the night. Even a light

shower could wash something that fragile away, or bury
it in the mud.

Without hesitation, she turned off the burner under the
stew she was preparing for supper and walked out of the
house. Heading for the worn trail that followed the bayou
for a short distance into the woods, her eyes scanned the
rutted ground around her, praying she'd spot a glimmer
of gold in the earth-brown mix of dried mud, leaves and
twigs, but she didn't see anything.

She continued on, carefully retracing her earlier steps.
Just as she had done all day long, she found her mind
wandering to the past, to the time when Cory had offered to marry her and of how grateful she had been. But
mostly she thought of Zachary and how easily she'd
fallen in love with him from the very start.

She was hopeless, she thought to herself, bending down
to study the shadows of a deep hole, thinking she'd seen
something shiny inside. But there was no sign of her
wristwatch.

She knew she would always love Zachary. A part of her
just couldn't let him go. But loving him was just something she would have to contend with in the silent sadness of her heart. There were too many secrets locked
away for her to think of doing otherwise. She had Alyse
to consider, and her pride—and Cory's memory. Besides, Zachary didn't have one ounce of feeling for her.
He probably never had.

She glanced around her surroundings, kicking her foot
through the overgrown brush, hoping to dislodge her
watch.

Keeping her eyes to the ground, she turned around,
deciding it was useless to go on. She didn't think she'd
even come this far earlier. Besides, shadows were al-

ready falling beneath the tall pines thickening the forest
and making it harder for her to see ahead.

Yet she hated to give up.

An abundance of wild blackberry bushes lined the
bayou bank, while various sorts of dark green vegeta-
tion grew closer in, covering the hard ground beneath the
brush. Other than a few singing birds, the forest lay silent, and the lonely sounds made by the mockingbirds
only added to her already melancholy mood. For some
reason their songs sounded so forlorn. Maybe it was because they, too, reminded her of the young love she and
Zac had once shared. It had been an afternoon much like
this when they'd made love for the first time. And it was
afterward, as she'd lain in his arms, that Zac had first
said he would love her forever.

The sudden soft rustling of dried debris snapped Lainie
from her thoughts. Quickly glancing to her left, she
searched the fallen pine needles for any sign of danger,
praying she wouldn't encounter a skunk—or, worse, a
poisonous snake. She exhaled with a sigh, smiling when
she spotted an armadillo scooting from one bush to another, knowing for just a second they'd shared a mutual
fear. It wasn't that she frightened easily, but she'd been
taught long ago not to take the unknown for granted.

Slowly she began to step forward, her eyes still scan-
ning the area nervously. At that moment the tip of her
yellow leather sandal caught on a hidden vine. Her right
hand reached out for a nearby tree, and she latched on to
its small trunk with her arm, hoping to prevent herself
from falling. A burning sensation on the side of her foot
preceded a thin line of blood that formed from her small
toe to her heel. She groaned lightly, realizing she should
have changed into her sneakers before coming out here.

She had taken only a few more steps when a shrill scream rent the heavy silence. She froze in place, her eyes widening. Was that a bear? No, bears didn't scream like that—did they?

She recalled being told numerous times that there weren't any more wild animals in these parts—at least, not any big, threatening ones—and with every drop of sweat covering her body, she desperately wanted to believe that was true. But, on the other hand, she vaguely recalled the few old-timers in the area who thought otherwise. Her mind conjured forth one image after another of some untamed beast lurking in the dense forest. Something as big and dangerous as a bear or a panther.

You're panicking for nothing, she told herself. There's nothing out there—except maybe a screech owl.

What's wrong with you? she continued. You're not usually spooked so easily. Yet all the while, as she tried reassuring herself, an eerie feeling crept up her spine. Her vivid imagination played havoc with her already frazzled nerves. She forced herself to breathe normally while every muscle in her body strained against moving. Her eyes darted from one side to the other, fearing some huge cat would jump for her throat at any second.

You're overreacting, she repeated silently over and over, yet that strange feeling of being watched tingled down her back. It's just an owl, she told herself once again, wanting to reassure herself but completely failing.

Just find your watch, silly, and stop acting like a child, she told herself.

Still apprehensive, she swallowed and took a half step back. The heel of her right foot sank into a deep hole. Waving her arms aimlessly, she fought for balance.

Despite her best effort, she landed flat on her back. A cry of surprise came out like a suppressed groan bubbling in her throat. The side of her head hit the base of a cypress tree with a thud. A sharp pain shot through her body and took what little breath she had left.

Disoriented, she moaned while grabbing her right ankle, for the moment forgetting her recent fear. One brief glance at her foot told Lainie the injury was serious. It had already doubled in size, and she stared in disgust as it seemed to grow larger.

Using her hands for support, she tried to stand but immediately realized she couldn't apply any pressure to her left wrist. Something made her feel the side of her head, and she discovered a lump the size of a small lemon.

Her breathing came in short quick gasps as though she'd been running a mile instead of merely attempting to rise. She felt nauseated and lay back on her elbows, staring at the overhead sky between the branches of the tall cypress. What a mess, she thought as perspiration trickled down her face and along the center of her back.

She could tell the sun was sinking fast by the orange glow peeking through the long skinny needles. She had to get up. It would be dark in less than an hour, and she knew no one would find her here. At least, not tonight.

"Don't panic," she said in a commanding voice. "You'll never get out of here before nightfall if you do."

Acknowledging that possibility heightened her fear. The prospect of spending the night as the easy prey for some wild animal was terrifying. A few years ago the old man who lived up the road had said wild boars still roamed these woods, but in all the years she'd lived here, Lainie didn't recall ever seeing one. Still, a chill teased the skin of her sweat-sodden body. Even if there weren't any bears or wild pigs, there were plenty of snakes in south Louisiana.

Once again she tried standing, but it was still useless. She couldn't walk. She felt dizzy. Sitting, she dragged herself to the cypress tree and leaned against its trunk.

"I'll crawl if I have to," she mumbled, rubbing her aching wrist and, at the same time, reminding herself that she wouldn't be in this predicament in the first place if she hadn't panicked.

Rolling onto her stomach, she placed her one good hand palm down on the ground and pushed herself into a kneeling position, forcing her foot to straighten out. The intense pain was more than she could stand. She screamed in anguish.

The trees were now casting deeper shadows around her. She willed herself to move by saying, "Come on, Lainie. One small crawl for man. One giant crawl for mankind."

Her strapless sundress caught under her knees, restricting her movements. In her frustration, she fought with the fabric, rolling it up and trying to tuck it out of the way. But her efforts failed, and the full skirt continued to tangle itself and impede her efforts. Her temper exploded in a flood of tears.

"Damn dress," she cried, lying on her side. Grabbing a handful of fabric, she tugged at the skirt until the seam at the waist gave. She ripped the fabric from the bodice, leaving only her sheer bikini panties to cover her delicate flesh. Now her long tanned legs were bared to insect bites and burning scratches. At the moment, though, she didn't care.

Tears and dust mingled together with makeup to form a muddy smear on her face, her hair was tangled from the twigs and leaves clinging to it, and her legs and arms bled from the nicks she received while dragging her weight along the ground.

She seemed to crawl for hours, stopping every so often to rest. At times she still felt nauseated and wondered if she didn't have a mild concussion.

The lonely sounds of insects at nightfall echoed around her. She no longer felt the bruising pain of her knees. She forced her bent legs forward, her only objective being to somehow reach home. But somewhere in the back of her mind she knew it was fruitless. She would never make it back tonight.

Still on her knees, completely worn-out, she dropped her head and sobbed. She'd never felt so helpless. Not even when she'd tried phoning Zac to tell him about the baby. At least then Cory had been there to help her. Yet even as she prayed for a rescuer, it wasn't Cory's face that loomed in her mind.

Oh, please . . . find me, she silently pleaded as images of haunting green eyes faded into blackness.

While driving back home, Zac pushed in a cassette and leaned back in his seat to think over his plan for getting even with Lainie.

He knew one thing for sure. His thoughts of revenge were in serious jeopardy. The hot flame of anger he'd felt when he learned of her well-kept secret was slowly becoming a flicker. Why?

It wasn't that he didn't still want justice, because he did. But did he really have the heart for what he intended? And if so, would Alyse understand and forgive him if he deliberately hurt her mother?

Suddenly there was so much to be considered. He was playing with people's lives—the very thing he'd accused Lainie of doing—and he wasn't sure anymore if the consequences were worth the price. Would he ever find peace within himself if he broke Lainie's spirit by seducing her, only to laugh in her face later? Or would the dull ache inside him only grow stronger until it smothered his own spirit?

He pulled up to the family homestead and found the house in darkness, as though no one was home. He frowned, wondering if Lainie had deliberately gone to bed this early in hopes of avoiding him. It would be just like her to do something like that. Well, if she had, he just might have to wake the lady up, he told himself.

He climbed out of the Jag and for a few seconds stood with his hands on his hips, staring at the darkened windows. Then he slammed the door, and the sound echoed through the quiet night. Still, he hesitated, trying to make sense of the scene before him.

Did Lainie think she could avoid him forever? he wondered, his anger fueled once again at the thought that she would go this far. Standing there and staring at her darkened window, his desire for sweet revenge renewed itself a fraction of a degree.

He noticed her car parked in the garage and frowned.

Maybe she had left with a friend—or maybe she had a date, the sneaky side of his brain said.

Bingo! he thought with a scornful expression fixed on his face. That would explain her sudden coolness toward him. Of course, she had a date tonight.

With who? he wondered. And where would they go? A motel? His gut felt as if it were being wrapped in barbed wire. Damn her. What was she trying to do to him?

No wonder she didn't want him here. He interfered with her personal life. Well, she was going to find out

about interference when she returned. He couldn't wait
to get his hands on her.

Jealous? his inner voice asked.

No, of course not, he argued back. Aggravated, but
certainly not jealous.

You sure? the voice whispered.

Yes—no—yes.

Come on, admit it, Benjamin, his inner voice per-
sisted. You're eaten alive with jealousy. Just think, he's
probably holding her, kissing her....

"Oh, blast. What's the use?" Zachary said aloud.
"Yes, I'm jealous, you lousy nag. Now are you satisfied
with yourself?"

Uh-huh, the little voice replied.

Gritting his teeth, Zachary stormed up the walk.

He fumbled around in the dark for the key he knew
was hidden nearby. In the meantime, his other hand came
to rest on the doorknob. One slight movement and he realized the door wasn't locked. That sparked his curiosity. Wouldn't she have locked the house?

He stepped inside. The house was as silent and as dark
as it had looked from the outside, except for moonlight
streaming in through the open drapes. A shiver ran down
the lean muscular length of Zac's body as he gazed
around the parlor.

Something was definitely wrong. He could feel it. The
old house was too quiet, too perfect. It reminded him of
an old black-and-white science fiction movie he'd seen as
a kid, when some kind of poisonous gas had escaped
from a truck and within minutes evaporated all the people in a nearby town.

He tried to remain calm as he walked from room to
room, flicking on lights. He called out Lainie's name in
each room, hoping for a reply. Nothing. After taking the

stairs two at a time, he rushed into her bedroom, only to find it empty, too.

"Lainie!" he yelled out, hoping she would spring out from behind a door, saying "Surprise," and throwing her arms around his neck. But she didn't.

Zac ran his fingers through his hair as his jean-covered legs took long strides over the worn blue carpet. A deep frown etched its way across his face when he smelled a hint of her floral perfume in the air. Had she been here just recently?

The door to the bath across the hall stood partially open, allowing the overhead light to drift into a small portion of the hallway. Without hesitation, he moved forward and pushed the door completely open, his heart thumping with anticipation. Disappointment washed over him. No Lainie.

He crossed back to her room in quick strides and carelessly yanked on the window shade; it rolled up with a loud fluttering sound. Although the window was swollen with age and usually had to be forced, he jerked it open with very little effort. He yelled Lainie's name into the blackening night. His stomach tightened when no one answered.

The distance between the first floor and himself was eaten up in quick steps that took him into the kitchen. Despite the spicy smell of cinnamon that permeated the room, Lainie's perfume still lingered along his senses. His emerald eyes searched the countertops. When he saw her purse sitting near the telephone, he couldn't shake the feeling that something was terribly wrong. A growing concern for her safety oozed into his every pore.

Maybe she had gone someplace with a friend, or maybe she *did* have a date, he thought, now ready to gladly admit that possibility in lieu of his other thoughts.

But surely she would have locked the house. The place was wide open, and her wallet was still in her leather bag he noted without a moment's regret for invading her privacy.

"Hell, I don't care how much Lainie claims to have changed," Zachary said aloud. "She wouldn't have left everything unlocked."

A scratching sound caused him to jerk his head toward the door. "Lainie?" he asked, his heart leaping into his throat. Without even waiting for a reply, he pulled it open, only to be disappointed once more. Morris stood there, panting.

"Where's your mistress, huh, boy?" Zac asked as if he expected the dog to answer him. He squatted down and ruffled the dog's fur. It was then that he noticed a glimmer just beneath the welcome mat.

He switched on the porch light. Morris licked at his hand as he tossed back one end of the small square rug. Discovering a wristwatch, he picked it up, examined it and recognized the piece of jewelry as belonging to Lainie. Clenching the small watch in his palm, he stared off into the dark night.

The forest looked as black as Cajun coffee.

Could Lainie have wandered into the woods? Or could an intruder have forced her into the darkness, causing her to lose her watch in the process?

He didn't even realize he was following the trail into the forest until he stumbled over a rut. Though he tripped a couple of times, he allowed nothing to slow him down, not even the burning sensations he felt from branches sticking into the flesh of his arms. The ragged sound of his breathing was loud in his ears as his anxiety over Lainie's welfare grew. He called her name.

Tall pines loomed in his path. With each step he took, the shrubs and trees grew thicker. His mind conjured up images of Lainie hurt and crying for help. Dear God, he thought while jogging deeper into the darkness, what's happened to her? Bile formed in his throat. Had she been attacked by some madman?

Why was it always the awful pictures that came to mind at a time like this?

He heard Morris bark and realized the dog had followed him along.

Suddenly he saw a body just a few feet in front of him. He halted, his heart ceasing to beat for a moment. Though the body lay prone to the ground, he knew it was Lainie.

"Oh—God—no," he said aloud, his worst fears confirmed.

Zachary groaned as he reached her, his mind wanting to deny what was happening. She was half-naked, and from what he could see, her delicate skin was scratched and bruised from head to toe.

He felt as if he were moving in slow motion, acting out a nightmare. Kneeling beside her, he placed his fingertips on her throat, searching for a pulse and fearing he'd find none.

He held his breath, his body leashed with tension. Morris stared into his face, and Zachary had never felt as close to an animal as he did to the big collie in that moment. Whether or not Morris understood what was happening was irrelevant to Zachary. He needed a friend right then.

There. He felt it. Yes, her pulse. "She's alive, boy," he whispered as a feeling of such strong relief washed over him that his eyes filled with tears. "God, she's alive," he said again, rejoicing in being able to say the words.

He wanted to turn her over onto her back, but first he had to be sure he wouldn't hurt her further. Using his hands, he carefully examined her for injury.

Slowly his fingers slid over her back and sides, gently probing as they moved down her legs, and finally feeling her arms for broken bones. He ran his hand once more down her leg, feeling the swelling of her right ankle.

Zachary steadied himself before slipping his left arm under her. Slowly he rolled her over onto his arm. It somehow registered that she was still wearing panties, but that was just about all except for a small piece of clothing still covering her chest. His free hand immediately began feeling her abdomen, applying just enough pressure to assess the extent of her injuries. What he found was smooth, silken skin marred by scratches and cuts.

His hands roamed across her full breasts, and he thought of how wonderful it would have been to have her moaning with pleasure instead of lying unconscious in his arms. All his insides seemed to ball up in the middle of his chest. If someone had hurt her, the animal responsible would pay.

His hand gently wiped away the dampened hair plastered to the sides of her face. He lightly brushed the dirt from her cheek. He leaned closer, his eyes soaking in what he could see of her features. Whispering her name, he touched his lips to hers.

Lainie responded with a moan. Her eyes slowly fluttered open, and Zachary witnessed the look of confusion, fear, then sheer relief moving across her face when she recognized him. Low sobs erupted from her throat, and her arms embraced his neck in a grip he wouldn't have thought her capable of in her condition.

"Oh, Zac," she cried, her voice breaking with sudden tears.

He held her tightly, whispering comforting words while his own tears mingled with hers. "Honey, it's okay. I've got you now. You're safe. It's all right," he assured her, cradling her in his arms as he stood. All he wanted at the moment was to get her home. He wasn't sure how badly she was hurt, and he certainly didn't want to upset her by asking her questions now.

She clung to him for several more seconds, before she lost consciousness. Pressing his lips to her forehead, he tasted the salty residue of sweat and grime. He found himself whispering words of comfort to her, words that came from his soul and spoke of his innermost feelings, the very ones he'd once tried to insist were no longer there.

Morris ran ahead and waited near the swing, wagging his tail and whining as Zac came forward carrying Lainie.

Managing to keep Lainie safely tucked in his arms, he opened the door to the house, then kicked it shut just as Morris scooted into the kitchen. "Stay, boy," Zac commanded.

Climbing the stairs, careful not to jar her, he carried Lainie into the bedroom and gently laid her down.

For a moment he just stared into her face. Then he turned and clicked on the bedside lamp.

What he saw made him want to yell out in anger. The palms of her hands and knees were bruised and bleeding. Scratches, some deep and some no more than a scrape, flawed her sensitive skin. Miraculously, other than two small nicks, her face appeared not to have suffered the same abuse, but there was a large lump on the side of her head.

He continued to check her carefully. Relief washed over him when he decided she hadn't been molested.

Nothing made any sense. It was obvious that her clothing had been ripped to shreds. Had she fought with someone and managed to get away? Had her assailant heard Morris and himself as they'd approached and run off?

It didn't matter, he told himself. She was safe now. Later the police could get involved.

He walked into the bathroom and wet a cloth. He couldn't trust Lainie's health to just his own observation. She needed a doctor. He decided to call his cousin, who had been Cory's doctor. Walking to her side, he leaned over and placed the cool cloth on her forehead.

A few moments later he took a deep breath, then exhaled slowly, picked up the phone and dialed the operator.

It didn't take long for him to reach Bryon and explain the situation. Their conversation was brief, ending with Bryon's assurance that Lainie was probably more shaken than anything else. But Zac had heard the urgency in Bryon's voice when he'd said he'd be right over.

While waiting for his cousin, Zac filled the sink with warm water, kept rewetting the cloth and began to wipe away the dried dirt from her face and arms. Then, using a small pair of scissors, he slid the point of one blade under what was left of Lainie's bodice and, in one move, ran the sharp cutting edge from her waist to her breast, baring her to his gaze.

The smooth texture of her skin looked as delicate as a wildflower, her dark dewy nipples as potent as bourbon whiskey, and while committing the image of her beauty to memory, he allowed his eyes to pour over her in loving reverence.

His eyes lifted to her face, and he found her watching him. Though weary, she attempted a smile. Zachary pulled his thoughts together and returned a half-hearted grin. One hand came to rest on her upper abdomen, just under her breast.

"Hi, sweetheart. Are you in pain?"

Lainie stared into his face without answering. Suddenly her mouth began to tremble, and her eyes glistened with renewed tears that rolled down her cheeks. Zachary ached from seeing her distress.

"Shhhh. Don't cry, sweetheart. It's okay," he said reassuringly. He used his long blunt fingers to wipe away her tears.

"I was so frightened," she choked out, her body beginning to shake.

"I know. But you're safe now," he said, his voice thick with emotion. He wanted to lie down beside her and warm her trembling body with his own. But he didn't dare trust himself to stop at just holding her. He leaned over, and in doing so, his shirt grazed the tips of her breasts, causing his own nipples to tighten into pebble hardness. Lainie's eyes widened in awareness of her nakedness, and she began protesting his efforts.

"No. Don't!" she exclaimed weakly, pushing at his hands. "What are you doing?"

Zachary grabbed her arms and held them back against the mattress. "Lainie, you've been hurt. I'm just cleaning your cuts. I've called Bryon. He's on his way."

Their eyes met and held. Slowly he relaxed his hold on her. Lainie's weakened condition gave him the advantage, and after several more attempts to brush his insistent hands away from her body, she closed her eyes and appeared to relax under his determined yet gentle ministrations.

She was beautiful. Even with the ugly red scratches marring her body, she was the loveliest creature ever

FREE BOOKS!

FREE GIFTS!

PLAY THE "LUCKY 7" SLOT MACHINE GAME !

NO COST! NO OBLIGATION TO BUY!
NO PURCHASE NECESSARY!

PLAY "LUCKY 7"
AND GET AS MANY AS SIX FREE GIFTS...

HOW TO PLAY:

1. With a coin, carefully scratch off the silver box at the right. This makes you eligible to receive one or more free books, and possibly other gifts, depending on what is revealed beneath the scratch-off area.

2. You'll receive brand-new Silhouette Romance™ novels. When you return this card, we'll send you the books and gifts you qualify for *absolutely free!*

3. If we don't hear from you, every month we'll send you 6 additional novels to read and enjoy. You can return them and owe nothing but if you decide to keep them, you'll pay only $2.25* per book, plus only 69¢ for delivery for the entire shipment!

4. When you join the Silhouette Reader Service™, you'll get our monthly newsletter, as well as additional free gifts from time to time just for being a subscriber.

5. You must be completely satisfied. You may cancel at any time simply by sending us a note or a shipping statement marked ''cancel'' or returning any shipment to us at our cost.

*Terms and prices subject to change.
© 1991 HARLEQUIN ENTERPRISES LIMITED

This lovely Victorian pewter-finish miniature is perfect for displaying a treasured photograph. And it's yours FREE as added thanks for giving our Reader Service a try!

PLAY "LUCKY 7"

Just scratch off the silver box with a coin.
Then check below to see which gifts you get.

YES! I have scratched off the silver box. Please send me all the gifts for which I qualify. I understand I am under no obligation to purchase any books, as explained on the opposite page.

315 CIS ACHD
(C-SIL-R-04/91)

NAME

ADDRESS   APT

CITY   PROV.   POSTAL CODE

7	7	7	WORTH FOUR FREE BOOKS, FREE VICTORIAN PICTURE FRAME AND MYSTERY BONUS
🍒	🍒	🍒	WORTH FOUR FREE BOOKS AND MYSTERY BONUS
●	●	●	WORTH FOUR FREE BOOKS
🔔	🔔	🍒	WORTH TWO FREE BOOKS

DETACH AND MAIL CARD TODAY

Business Reply Mail

No Postage Stamp
Necessary if Mailed
in Canada

Postage will be paid by

SILHOUETTE
READER SERVICE
P.O. Box 609
Fort Erie, Ontario
L2A 9Z9

Canada Post
Postes Canada
125

DETACH AND MAIL CARD TODAY

created, and for a moment he forgot all else. He wanted only to take her in his arms and kiss away her every pain. What an idiot he'd been to think he could ever hurt her in any way.

Bending forward, he placed his lips just above her navel.

It had been twenty years since he'd been able to physically love her. And not for one single moment in all those twenty years had he stopped longing to do just that—and he'd been a complete fool to think otherwise. No woman had ever come close to fulfilling him as completely as Lainie had. Even now, when he wasn't sure that she didn't despise him, he wanted her and needed her more than any other human being.

He'd missed it all. The great Zachary Benjamin. The guy who was envied by his peers for his talent and success had never experienced the simple joy of being a husband to the woman he loved and a father to his only child.

He heard footsteps on the stairs just before Bryon called out to him. He quickly covered Lainie, carefully tucking the blanket beneath her arms and along her sides.

He stood. Unexpectedly, Lainie's hand reached up in search of his.

"Please don't leave me alone, Zac," she said, gripping his hand. "I don't want to be alone."

"It's okay, sweetheart. I'm not going to leave you," he whispered, squeezing her hand reassuringly before placing a kiss on her palm.

Would he keep that promise? he wondered, as he glanced up and found Bryon standing in the doorway.

Chapter Six

In the distance Lainie could hear the humming of the ceiling fan and the murmuring of male voices. It reminded her of a hospital, of the times she'd awakened during the night to the quiet humming of the air-conditioning unit in Cory's room and listened intently for his breathing.

She tried turning on her side, but a sharp pain stopped her. Every bone in her body ached. Every muscle begged to be left alone.

Using one hand as **a** support, she tried to rise. "Uuuuhh!" she moaned, biting her lower lip.

"Don't move, Lainie."

The commanding voice had come from Zachary as he placed his wide hands on her shoulders and forced her back against the mattress.

Lainie slowly became aware of her surroundings, and after sweeping her eyes across the room, she settled them on the worried-looking face only a couple of feet away.

A shadow of alarm crossed her features. Fatigue had worked its way into the small lines around Zac's eyes, making him look exhausted.

The realization that he cared enough about her to have it show touched some fine-tuned emotion deep within her.

Maybe he *had* lied to her all those years ago. Maybe he *hadn't* cared what happened to her back then. But tonight he cared. She would have to be blind not to see the open feelings chiseled into the handsome face looming over her. As she gazed at him, a slow, reassuring smile lifted the corners of his mouth.

He sat next to her on the edge of the bed, took her hand and turned it so he could examine the palm. "Do your hands hurt?"

Without answering him, she freed herself from his grasp and without hesitation ran her fingers through the dark hair that had fallen over his forehead.

"You look worried. Don't be. I'm okay now."

The sad, bittersweet curve of her mouth rocked the world under his feet. It was like being given a penny's worth of sunshine when he'd thought there was none left to be found.

Finding his wayward voice, he said, "Don't worry about me. Bryon's here to check you over—make sure everything is okay."

"I'm just bruised," Lainie mumbled, gliding her tongue over her dry lips. Her throat hurt. "But I'm thirsty."

As though he'd known what she would say, Bryon tapped Zachary on the shoulder and handed him a paper cup filled with tap water. "Best let me be the judge of how you are," he said. "I know how hardheaded you can be about things like this."

Lainie lifted herself up, and Zachary placed his arm around her back, giving her the necessary support to drink from the cup he held to her lips.

She sipped the water, her eyes rising to meet his. "Thanks," she whispered in a hoarse voice as he lowered her to the pillows.

Bryon motioned for Zachary to move aside. Without hesitation, the doctor sat on the bed next to her, lifted one eyelid and flashed a light into the pupil. Then he did the same to the other. Afterward he adjusted his stethoscope to his ears and gave Lainie the grin that made him so popular with patients and friends alike. "Did you get in a fight with a blackberry bush?"

Lainie glanced from Bryon to Zachary. Neither of them fooled her. Unleashed tension filled Zachary's body as he stood only a few feet behind his cousin, and Bryon's voice had lacked the humor he'd intended.

"Take a deep breath," he said while listening to her lungs. "Now another... and another." Finally he pulled the stethoscope from his ears. "What happened to you?"

"I... I fell."

"We know that," Bryon said. "But how did you fall?"

"Were you chased? Forced?" Zachary asked, clenching his fists at his sides. He was ready to avenge any wrong that had been done to her. None of this would be happening if only he hadn't gone into town. What an idiot he'd been. No matter what wrong she'd done him in the past, he still loved her, and he couldn't stand to see her in pain.

"No, it wasn't anything like that."

"Then what were you running from?" he asked anxiously.

From my love for you, Lainie thought. Instead she replied, "Nothing."

"Were you hiding in the woods from someone? One of those guys you mentioned the other morning just before you burned your fingers on the toaster. You never did tell me who—"

"No, Zachary. Of course not," Lainie said, sounding frustrated.

"You're upsetting her, Zac. Let's just drop it for now, okay?" Bryon said.

"Yeah—sure," Zachary mumbled, shaking his head and feeling like a fool. It was just that he couldn't tolerate the idea of someone trying to hurt her. He turned and walked out of the bedroom, closing the door behind him. Maybe it would be better if he just waited downstairs. His nerves were shot, and what he really needed at the moment was a good, strong drink.

Thirty minutes later, Bryon stood unnoticed at the foot of the stairs and watched his cousin's movements. He wished there was something he could do to help ease the strain between Lainie and Zac, but for the life of him, he couldn't think of anything. Maybe time was the only answer.

While Bryon had been examining her, Lainie had told him that Zachary was home for a rest and that he wanted them to become friends again. Bryon wasn't sure what that meant, but he wondered if they could become just friends after all that had happened over the years.

And, too, he couldn't help but worry whether Zachary had an ulterior motive for being here. If so, Bryon wondered, what could it be? Zac might have been his cousin, but Lainie was his friend, and he didn't want to see her hurt.

But if the two of them *could* become friends, Bryon felt it would probably be for the best. After all, they were

family. And if by chance something more were to de-
velop, he knew for a fact that Cory would have been
pleased. Once, just after learning about his illness, Cory
had told him that he thought his cancer was fate's way of
taking him out of Lainie's life. Lord knew she never
would have left him—not even for Zachary. It was a tri-
angle Cory had often discussed with Bryon through the
years. Zachary loved Lainie. Or had. Cory loved Lainie.
And Lainie loved them both, in different ways, but it was
love just the same. All the years. All the pain. Could the
two people Cory adored really make peace with themselves and with each other?

Bryon stepped forward. "You can stop turning yourself inside out. I don't think any of her injuries are serious. She didn't have a concussion, like I'd originally
thought. The lump on the side of her head is already
going down. She should be okay in a few days, but to be
on the safe side, bring her to the hospital at about nine in
the morning. Her right ankle does look pretty bad, and
one of her wrists is swollen, too. I'll leave orders for both
of them to be X-rayed." Bryon set his medical bag on the
sofa and glanced at his watch. "It's already after mid-
night."

Zachary inhaled deeply. "Yeah, it's late. Look, I must
have sounded a little crazy when I called. Thanks for
coming so quickly."

"You certainly didn't sound like the coolheaded star
everyone thinks you are, if that's what you mean," Bryon
said with a hint of amusement. "You were pretty upset."

"Is she sleeping, now?"

"No, but she will be soon, and she probably won't
awaken until morning. I gave her a mild sedative. She's
exhausted and needs the rest."

Zachary nodded in agreement. "Should she stay in bed—off her ankle?"

"Definitely. If it's just sprained, she'll need to be off it for a few days, possibly a week. But if there's a fracture, she'll be in a cast. Her scratches will just take time to heal. Her left wrist is probably sprained. But as far as I can tell without X rays, her ankle is her worst injury," Bryon said, removing his glasses and rubbing his eyes with the palm of his hand.

"Did she tell you what happened? Should we call the police?"

"No. The police won't be necessary. Lainie managed to do all that to herself."

Zachary stared at Bryon as if he had just appeared out of thin air. "What the devil is that supposed to mean?"

"It seems she'd gone for a short walk along the bayou this afternoon and lost her watch."

"I found it," Zac said, remembering the watch for the first time since he'd picked it up and tucked it into his pocket. "It was under the mat by the back door."

"Well, she said she looked everywhere, and when she didn't find it in the house, she went back along the bayou to search for it, all the while knowing it was going to be dark soon. Anyway, she heard some kind of a scream, probably nothing more than a screech owl. But she panicked and stepped into a hole, causing her ankle to turn. She fell flat on her back. She tried to get up, but she couldn't put any pressure on the ankle. She was afraid no one would find her until morning, so she tried crawling on her good hand and her knees until her energy gave out. That's how she got most of her scratches."

"That's pretty incredible. Sounds like a soap opera to me," Zachary commented in an argumentative tone.

"Are you sure she's not trying to protect some jerk who's been after her?"

Bryon bowed his head. He hoped Zachary hadn't seen the smile crossing his face. His cousin had actually sounded jealous, and the guy hadn't even realized it. So he did still care for Lainie. That explained a lot of the tension he'd felt between them. Neither one wanted the other to know their true feelings.

If the night hadn't been so crazy, it would have been funny. Boy, wouldn't the gossip magazines have a field day with this? Bryon could see the headlines now: Zachary Benjamin's Jealousy Over Widowed Sister-In-Law's Phantom Lover. He couldn't help himself when he saw Zac's bewildered expression. He laughed out loud.

Zachary closed the door behind his cousin. Bryon had finally managed to convince him that Lainie wouldn't have protected anyone who could do such a thing to her.

He climbed the stairs slowly as the day's events raced across his mind.

Nothing was coming easily for him. Hating Lainie was fast proving to be an impossible task—one he was beginning to doubt he could pull off. And yet, admitting he still loved her was proving to be equally impossible. How could he forgive all the wrong she'd done him?

He pulled the watch from his pocket and examined it closely. The inscription on the back read *Everlasting, Cory.*

What would his brother say if he knew of his plan to get even with Lainie? Would he slowly shake his head from side to side the way he always did as a kid when something didn't meet his approval? Or, as a man, had he handled such situations differently? Zachary realized that unless someone told him, he would never know the answer to that question, because he had never gotten to know the man his younger brother had become.

Climbing the stairs, he closed his hand tightly over the watch and let the pain stabbing at his heart make all the wounds it wanted.

He went into his bedroom and tossed his cap on the bedpost before walking into the bathroom. He laid the watch on top the counter next to one of her bracelets. Tomorrow he would tell her where he had found it. With the inscription still on his mind, he turned on the shower and peeled off his dirty clothes.

Leaving the door to Lainie's room ajar, he stepped into the tub. The pulsating water from the shower head felt great as he lathered his body with clean, fresh-smelling soap. Every few minutes he opened the shower door, stuck his wet head out and checked on his patient. As of yet, she hadn't moved.

He turned off the water, reached out and grabbed a big fluffy towel from the shelf. Briskly rubbing his head, he gathered the thing to his nose and sniffed. Baby powder. The darn thing smelled like baby powder. A picture of Lainie nursing his daughter at her breast flashed through his mind and tightened his stomach.

He wrapped the towel around his waist and stared into the mirror while rubbing one side of his jaw, then the other. His beard felt stubby. More from habit than anything, he ran his fingers through his dark hair, then glanced once more toward her bedroom. She still hadn't moved.

He walked to her bedside, allowing his eyes to touch her face. It was a gentle gaze, as soft and tender as a lover's caress. His heart constricted. Did she have a reason for breaking her promise to him all those years ago? He suddenly found himself wanting to believe she did.

He watched the hypnotic rise and fall of her chest. She looked so innocent and fragile, so sincere and incapable of deliberately duping anyone. For the moment he could almost forget all the pain she'd caused. But he couldn't forget the swell of her full breasts or the curve of her slim hips as he'd cleaned her wounds earlier tonight. Sudden desire spread through his body like brushfire in a hayfield. Liar—cheat—whatever she was, he still wanted her.

"Zac?"

"Yeah?" he answered quickly, huskily. His entire body responded to the sound of her soft voice in all the ways he'd wanted to deny. His heart pounded, causing his blood to surge through his veins. As their eyes met in the dim light, his brain echoed the memory of her long-ago promise of love.

The moment was so potent he couldn't breathe.

Nor could he touch her. Not now. Not when he had so little control over his actions.

"Zac, I need someone to hold me. I feel so alone...."

"Oh, baby," he said, leaning over her.

Their eyes met and locked as he smoothed back the fine hair spread across her forehead. "Lainie, I..." He hesitated. "I'll stay with you all night if you'd like."

He waited for her answer, and it came as no surprise to realize that if she rejected him now, he would bleed to death as surely as if his heart had been torn from his body.

"I want you to stay," she said in a trembling voice.

He didn't speak for fear of breaking the spell around them.

Slowly, gently, he slid onto the bed alongside her. "I won't hurt you if I lie down like this and slip my arm behind your head, will I?" he asked, his voice fading as his eyes tenderly traced the outline of her body.

"No." Her voice was strained, almost breathless.

Zac sensed the uncertainty in her, and when he saw her eyes glistening with tears, he knew she was as vulnerable as he was.

"Lainie, I swear I won't hurt you," he heard himself say, and—for the moment—he realized he meant every word.

Lainie bit her bottom lip to stop its quivering. The hunger that had been eating at her for twenty years cruised through her veins. In the past, just the thought of him making love to her had been enough to sustain her battered heart. But no more. Suddenly she realized she needed more than bittersweet memories. She needed Zac physically, spiritually, in every way a woman needs a man.

His large hands cradled her hips as Zachary inched his rigid torso closer to hers. With one arm around her slim shoulders and the other hand sliding to the small of her back, he eased her pliant body to his.

She looked into his emerald eyes, knowing their effect on her would be earth-shattering. "I don't want to be alone, Zac. I guess that makes me weak, but I don't want to be alone—not tonight," she whispered, gripping the tight muscles of his arm as flesh pressed against flesh.

"No, baby. It only makes you human. Come here," he said, his voice deep and filled with emotion. Positioning her against him, he rolled onto his back, making himself a cushion for her body as she pressed against his side.

Lainie squeezed her eyes shut against the pain of her bruised body, but soon she began to relax as Zac lifted her hair from her shoulders and spread it across his chest.

"Go to sleep. We'll talk in the morning. And don't worry about a thing," he added, placing his lips to her forehead. "I won't leave you tonight."

Slowly Lainie's hand slipped over his taut stomach until her arm encircled his waist. She breathed in the clean scent of him. "You smell clean . . ." she mumbled. "Like soap."

Within minutes, her breathing evened out and Zac knew the sedative she'd been given had taken full effect. He lay there for a long time, fighting his raging desire for her and wishing things could have been different between them.

He knew it was impossible for all the missing pieces of their lives to fit back together. Too much had happened. Yet, for the moment, he didn't care, nor did he have any answers about what would become of their future. But even if it would never happen again, for this one special night Lainie was sleeping in his arms, and though he hated to admit it to himself, he knew it was something he'd dreamed of as long as he cared to remember. Long before he ever had thoughts of revenge.

Dawn was barely breaking as the first rays of sunlight streamed through the open drapes. Zachary sat in the rocker next to Lainie's bedroom window and stared out. With the coming of morning, last night seemed more than ever like a dream.

Yet it wasn't, and, heaven help him, he wanted to hold her in his arms night after night and feel the softness of her body pressed to his. Stealing a quick glance in her direction, he found her still asleep.

When he had awakened a couple of hours ago from the best slumber he had had in ages, he had climbed out of her bed, only to face the fact that he had lost sight of his purpose.

He didn't need the tender feelings for her that haunted him. He didn't need them at all. They simply didn't fit into his plans. His emotions were raging out of control and complicating his plans—no, destroying his plans would be a better description. What in the world was he going to do? The thought of cancelling his mission of revenge in the name of love scared the daylights out of him. He hadn't come prepared for that.

How could he have let this happen? Of course Lainie felt good in his arms. Of course she looked innocent and helpless. Couldn't all women look that way when they needed to? Hadn't Lainie pulled that scam on him once before? Was he going to let her do it again?

He turned his eyes in her direction. She was facing him in sleep, and the floral sheet covering her slim body had slipped, so that he could see her full breasts. He wanted her. That was something he couldn't change, but then, he realized, he really didn't have to. What he had to do was get control of it and use it to his advantage. No more of this hanky-panky, let me hold you tonight stuff—unless it was part of his plan. That way he wouldn't lose sight of his objective the way he'd done last night.

With a confident smile on his face, he got up, adjusted his jeans and walked over to her bed. Her complexion was flawless, her mouth full and inviting. Every pore in his body yearned for the fulfillment he knew he'd find in her arms. But with a lot of effort on his part, he knew he could handle the temptation of physical desire. It was the yearning for something more that constantly sapped his confidence. But he could handle that, too, he told himself.

In one brisk move, he turned away and walked out her bedroom door. What he needed, he told himself, was a cup of strong, black Cajun coffee.

Something had interrupted her dreamlike state and was now bordering on becoming a total nuisance. That something had just crawled across her upper lip, making her mouth and nose twitch in protest, but still she resisted coming fully awake. Instead she groaned and turned onto her back, wiping her hand over her face. This time the something feather-walked across her forehead and then her chin.

"Mmmm," she moaned, still too dazed to think clearly. She swatted at the intrusion. It ignored her and zipped lightly across her upper lip. Again she groaned in protest.

"Tickles?"

"Uh-huh."

"Then wake up, sleepyhead. Your breakfast is getting cold."

"My what?" Lainie asked after a second, opening one eye, then the other. She stared for the longest time at the tray of food Zachary held, using those few precious moments to come fully awake. Finally her thoughts fell into place and memories of the previous night crowded her mind. She glanced quickly around the room and recognized it as her own.

Before she could speak, a loud ringing broke the silence.

Reaching for the phone, she glanced from Zachary to the window. The sun shone brightly through the curtains.

"Hello?"

"Lainie, it's Bryon. Just calling to remind you of your X ray. I have it set up here at the hospital for nine."

"X ray? What X ray?"

"Didn't Zachary tell you?"

She turned her eyes to Zac. "Tell me what?"

"I want an X ray of your ankle—just to be sure it isn't broken."

She lowered her gaze. "Oh, Bryon, for heaven's sake, that's not necessary. I know it's not broken. It's hardly even swollen anymore." She tried to move it, but found the pain too great.

"Yes it is, Bryon," Zachary said loudly, understanding the conversation and wanting his voice to override Lainie's. "Swelling like that takes a long time to go down. And it's purple, too."

The look Lainie gave Zac was so heated that it could have melted steel. "It is not," she said defiantly.

"You need an X ray, Lainie, and that's all there is to it," Bryon said seriously.

"I'll have her dressed and there in no time," Zachary interjected. "She just needs to eat her breakfast first."

Lainie didn't know which man to argue with, so she didn't argue with either. "Oh, all right. But just one."

"Yes, ma'am," Bryon answered cheerfully. "I'll see you two at the hospital."

She hung up and looked at Zac. "Why didn't you tell me about the X ray?"

"I was going to do just that."

Lainie looked again at the tray of food. "You didn't have to go to so much trouble. I could've gone downstairs."

"It wasn't any trouble. Of course, the kitchen doesn't look so hot."

He set the tray down on the table next to the bed and helped her sit up before placing her breakfast over her lap.

She looked down at her plate of ham, eggs, wheat toast, orange juice and coffee. "I can't eat all this."

"Yes, you can. Besides, you're going to need all the strength you can get to hobble around on one foot for a while."

"I really don't think my injury is that serious."

"You don't, huh?" he said, reaching over and throwing back the cover so she could get a glimpse of her foot. "See for yourself."

She stretched the top half of her body over her tray.

"Careful," Zac said when she bumped her glass of orange juice, almost toppling it. He reacted before she did and saved her from being drenched.

Gazing at her foot, she raised her eyebrows in concern. "I guess you're right. It does look pretty bad. Do you think it's just sprained?"

"We won't know for sure until it's X-rayed," he said.

"I can't go to the hospital looking like this. I need to clean up first."

Zachary smiled. "You looked a lot worse last night."

Remembering the gentle way he'd wiped away the dirt from her naked body, Lainie blushed. "Thanks for all you did."

"What are friends for?"

For a moment her eyes met and held his.

She hadn't wanted them to be friends in the beginning. But despite her best efforts, she found herself slowly warming toward him. Could they actually become as close as she and Cory had been?

Her heart leaped at the thought, but then she realized that was impossible. She and Cory had complemented each other, and that was what had made their relationship so special. She and Zachary simply tantalized each other, and that was what had kept their relationship a roller-coaster ride that never seemed to slow down.

"I found your watch."

"You did? Where? When?" she asked, the joy she felt evident in her voice.

"Last night, when I got home. It was under the back-door mat. I bent down to pat Morris, and there it was. Of course, I didn't know at the time you'd gone to look for it."

Lainie recalled what Zachary had thought and blushed. "I'm sorry if I worried you."

He shrugged. "It's no big deal. That watch must be very special to you."

She nodded. "Cory gave it to me."

"Yeah," Zachary replied huskily. "I saw the inscription."

Lowering her eyes, she lifted the glass of orange juice and took a swallow.

Once she finished breakfast, Zachary took the tray from her lap and said, "I'll bring this downstairs, and then I'll help you get to the bathroom so you can clean up."

"I think I can manage alone."

"Stay in bed until I get back," he said in a commanding voice.

He was back within a couple of minutes to help her into the long bathrobe she insisted on wearing. Then he carried her into the bath and sat her on the edge of the tub. "By the way, I put your watch right here," he said, pointing to the counter.

"Thanks," she replied, adjusting her hips on the white porcelain rim as he began placing the necessary toiletries near her. Then, putting his hands on his hips, he looked down at her, a mocking slant to his grin. "Gonna need any help?"

Her eyes skittered away from his. "No, I'll be fine," she said, turning on the faucets.

"You sure? I don't mind helping."

"I'm sure."

"Okay," he said. "If that's the way you feel . . . but if you change your mind, I'll be right in here," he said, backing toward the door.

She nodded.

He stopped in the doorway. "Yell if you need anything."

"I won't need anything," she said, reaching up to get the bottle of shampoo he had forgotten to put near her. But as fate would have it, she lost her balance, slid off the narrow edge and fell with a splash into the partially filled tub, soaking her long robe and drenching the floor around her. For a second she just sat there with a stunned expression on her face.

Zac tried not to laugh at the picture she made, but he couldn't help himself. "So you don't need any help, huh?"

"How can you laugh at a time like this?" she asked, not finding one thing funny about the situation.

His smile faded a fraction—but only a fraction. "You didn't hurt yourself, did you?"

"No, I didn't—no thanks to you."

"Me? How did I make you fall in the tub?"

"Because . . . because it took you so long to leave."

"You slipped because you refused my help. That's not *my* fault," he said, still grinning. He offered her his hand. "Come on. Looks like you need my help after all."

"I can manage by myself." Still sitting in the water, she began to struggle with the belt tied at her waist, but the wet fabric wouldn't respond.

"Here, let me help," he said, bending down to her level.

"I said I can do it myself."

Straightening, he placed his hands on his hips. "Are you or are you not going to let me help you get out of that robe?"

She tilted her chin up. "I don't need your help."

"In that case, you may end up having to bathe with your clothes on."

"That's fine with me," she replied.

He stood, then threw up his hands. "Women!" he exclaimed before walking out the door.

Chapter Seven

Lainie managed to bathe without his help and then wrapped herself in the large towel he'd placed within her reach. She was ready for him to enter when, several minutes later, he knocked lightly on the door.

He stopped short when he saw her sitting there with only a towel for clothing, her creamy skin glowing from the scrubbing she'd given herself. Slowly his narrowed gaze raked over her, raising his body temperature to a fever pitch. Did she have any idea what she was doing to him? Maybe he should point out the physical evidence to her—if she hadn't noticed for herself.

She had, and now, in order to breathe, she needed more oxygen.

Where do you hobble to when you want to get away from someone and you have only one good ankle and no place to go?

You don't, her brain reminded her. You sit there and act like nothing in the world is bothering you. If possible, smile.

She managed a weak grin.

Zachary was slowly inching his way back into her life, and she knew it. How could she stop him? And how could she stop herself from letting it happen? Didn't she have any defenses against him? Couldn't she fight him and win? After all, he was just a man, for heaven's sake.

But what a man, her brain reminded her.

It would be so easy for her to get used to having him around. At times she could almost pretend their lives had turned out differently. But then there was Alyse. Her daughter had adored Cory, and learning the truth of her conception at this stage in her life could be traumatic. No, Lainie thought, ignoring the pang of guilt that always accompanied thoughts of Alyse and Cory—and Zachary. She had done the right thing all those years ago. That one lie might have altered the paths their lives took, but it had saved her daughter from being labeled Zachary Benjamin's unwanted, illegitimate child. Back then, that had been her one and only concern, and if given a second chance, she was certain she would do things the same way again.

"What are you thinking about?" Zac asked, handing her another robe he found hanging on a hook in the bathroom.

"Nothing . . . nothing important."

He helped her into the robe, then lifted her up and carried her to the bed. "Do you have something loose to wear, like an old jogging suit?" he asked. "That would be the easiest thing to put on."

"The one I have needs laundering. But I have a pair of old baggy jeans hanging in my closet."

"I'll get 'em," he said.

"I'm sorry I'm so much trouble. I'm really grateful for all your help."

Something in her tone seemed to be trying to make a point. Narrowing his eyes, he turned in her direction. "What do you mean?"

"Well . . ." Lainie said hesitantly. "I know I told you I didn't want you here—but, well . . . you've been so help-ful that I—"

"Don't bother to say it," Zachary replied sarcasti-cally. "I think I get the picture. You're willing to toler-ate my presence as a gesture of appreciation." He jerked a pair of jeans from a hanger inside her closet and tossed them into her lap. "Well, don't do me any favors. I don't need your gratitude, Mrs. Benjamin. Not that kind, anyway."

Lainie grabbed her jeans and began struggling into one leg, but her sore wrist and swollen ankle hampered her efforts. Still, she wasn't about to ask for help. Not from him.

How could he? She'd only been trying to say she was sorry for acting the way she had toward him. Well, so much for being nice.

From the corner of his eye, Zachary watched her ef-forts to get into her jeans. What had made him so defen-sive a few moments ago? It wasn't like him to be that way. So she was grateful. Maybe he could use it to his advantage. "Here," he said, strolling toward her. "Lie back and let me do that for you. I've had lots of practice with snaps and zippers."

"I'll just bet you have," Lainie replied, a note of sar-casm in her voice. She had no idea what had possessed her to say that. Even to herself, she sounded like a jeal-ous wife.

Zac's head had snapped up at her quick comeback. "Now what is that suppose to mean? You keep dropping these little innuendos. Get to the point. What's bothering you?"

Trembling inside, Lainie took a deep breath. "Nothing's bothering me. It's just that I've read about your reputation with the ladies. Believe me, the magazines were quite explicit."

His eyes glistening with fury, he towered over her. "Although some of what you read or heard was probably the truth or close to it, I don't have to explain my actions to you." His voice was cold. "You married my brother, remember?"

Anger seized hold of her. Had he returned her calls, she wouldn't have had to marry Cory and get both of them involved in her web of lies. But now to tell Zac that would be to reveal her reason for phoning him in the first place. "Don't you dare say anything about Cory."

"I'm not saying anything about him. It's you I'm talking about. You and me. Remember that part of your life?"

Remember? She'd never forgotten one single minute of it. "Vaguely."

He jerked her from the bed and pinned her to him in one fluid motion. "Then maybe I ought to freshen up your memory."

In one tenth of a second, long before she knew what was coming, his lips crushed down on hers.

She wanted to scratch his eyes out and quickly decided she was going to do just that when she got loose from his tight hold.

She squirmed, trying to free herself. He didn't budge, didn't even loosen his grip on her.

She hated him. She hated herself. She hated fate for bringing them back together after so many years of pain. Hadn't she suffered enough?

Suddenly he released her lips and laid her back against the mattress. Bracing his hands on each side of her, he glared into her eyes.

Her hand snaked out and slapped him across the face. His expression never changed, his eyes never left hers, as he slowly rose to a standing position. "Now you listen, and listen good. I may be a lot of things, but I'm no cheat. I didn't become involved with another woman until way after you and Cory were married."

"You expect me to believe that when all the papers—"

His features turned to stone. "I don't give a damn what the newspapers said. You're just trying to blame me for something you did."

"That's a lie!" Lainie screamed.

"Like hell it is."

"Get out of my room."

He glared at her for a few more moments. Then, pivoting on his heel, he strode out the door. With tears burning her eyes, she finished dressing.

Zachary stormed back in several minutes later and whisked her up into his arms. In silence he carried her briskly to his car, which he'd pulled up to the front of the house. Silence was just fine with her. She had nothing more to say to him at the moment. It was bad enough that she was forced to rely on his help in order to get to the hospital.

By the time they reached the outpatients' entrance, it was past nine-thirty. Zac pulled up, braked and was out of his car in a flash, slamming the door behind him. The windows rattled from the force of it. Lainie pretended not to notice.

Without saying a word, he walked to her door, opened it and bent inside, then slipped one arm under her knees and the other behind her back. In seconds she was out of her seat and against his chest. Surprised, she sucked in her breath, her arms automatically encircling his neck.

"Hold on," he said, kicking the door shut with his booted foot before strolling up the flower-lined walkway.

"It isn't necessary for you to carry me like this," she said angrily.

"Don't give me a hard time about anything, Lainie. I've had enough of your arguments for one day."

She heard the threat in his voice. His jaw was clenched tightly. She didn't say another word. After all, she wasn't totally stupid.

Suddenly two attendants zoomed out the wide doorway, one pushing a wheelchair. "Here, mister. Set her in the chair."

"That's okay."

"But hospital policy—"

"I don't care about hospital policy. I'm carrying the lady inside."

"Hey! You're Zachary Benjamin. Hot dog—I'd know you anywhere," said the second attendant. "My dad said he played basketball with you in high school—before you were famous and all."

"Oh, yeah? Who's your father?" Zachary asked, ignoring the wheelchair as he continued walking.

"Mike Ardoin."

"No kidding. You're Mike's kid?"

"Yes, sir. I'm just working here for the summer. I graduated from high school this year. I'm going to LSU in the fall. Got an athletic scholarship."

"Gonna follow in your old man's shoes, huh? I bet Mike's proud of you. I know I would be—if a kid of mine followed in my footsteps," Zac said. His arms tightened around Lainie.

You do have a child! Lainie screamed silently. And she just might very well follow in your footsteps. But he doesn't know that, her brain told her. You've never told him, remember?

"Yes, sir. He's real proud," the lanky young man continued.

"Where is Mrs. Benjamin supposed to go?" Zac asked. "She's scheduled for an X ray."

As they entered the emergency room, Lainie gazed around. The small lobby quickly filled with white uniforms. Apparently the hospital staff had been expecting Zachary to bring her in. Surely the extra people standing around weren't necessary to X-ray one swollen ankle.

"My Lord, child, what's happened to you?"

Lainie's head turned toward the approaching figure. She recognized the short, plump woman right away. Before volunteering her help at the hospital, Joanna Bell had been the school nurse at Harrington High for thirty years. "It's nothing, Mrs. Bell. I hurt myself late yesterday afternoon. Bryon thinks my ankle needs an X ray to be sure it isn't broken."

With her hands on her hips, the stern-faced nurse glared at Zachary. "And I suppose you had nothing to do with this—just like when you were young. You were always into mischief, but you never had to take the blame."

"Now, Nurse Bell, don't you ever forgive and forget? I wasn't really *that* bad, was I?" Zac gave her a grin that seemed to turn back the clock to a time when he'd been a mischievous teen.

"You're right. You were worse. Cory was the good one. You—" she said, pointing to Zac "—were the troublemaker—always the troublemaker. I've patched you up more times than I can count."

Zachary gave her an exasperated look. "Well, could we forget about all that right now? The patient in my arms is beginning to get heavier with each passing second. You can complain about me all you want once I put her down," he added with that lopsided grin of his. "Where is she supposed to go?"

"Over here," came a familiar male voice. Bryon stood in a doorway several yards down the wide hall. He smiled as they came forward. "Our Nurse Bell giving you a hard time?"

"To say the least."

"Actually, she's a big fan of yours. Brags all the time about the pranks you conned Cory into playing on her."

"No kidding," Zachary replied. "Well, I'll be. You'd never know it by the way she acts. I'm glad not all my fans are like her. I wouldn't know if they were friend or foe."

"Set Lainie over here," Bryon said, smiling. Then, pointing to an open doorway, he continued, "You and I can wait in there while the technician does the X ray." Looking at the patient, he asked, "How does your ankle feel today?"

"Better. Much better. I don't think it's broken."

"And your wrist?"

"That's better, too," she said, exercising it for his benefit.

After a careful examination, he said, "Well, we'll know soon. Zachary and I will wait out here. It shouldn't take long."

Bryon was right. It took all of five minutes before the technician completed the picture taking. A few minutes later, Lainie was helped into a wheelchair and rolled down the hall by a slender nurse.

"Dr. Hebert is in there reading your X rays. He'll be out as soon as he's finished. Can I get you something?" the nurse asked when they came to a pair of swinging doors.

"No, I'm fine."

Bryon walked in a couple of minutes later. "Well, I hate to be the bearer of bad tidings, but your ankle *is* fractured. Right about here," he said, bending down and running his finger lightly along the outside of her leg.

Lainie followed his movements. "What does that mean?"

"That means you'll need a cast."

"Crutches?"

"I'm afraid so."

"Oh, for heaven's sake."

"They're not so bad once you get the hang of them. But for the next few days, I think it's best if you stay off it completely. Your wrist is just strained."

Lainie frowned. "So now what?"

"So now we put your ankle in a cast."

Lainie glanced around the room. She had expected to see Zac follow right behind Bryon, and, though she hated to admit it, it bothered her that he hadn't. "Where's Zachary?"

"He'll be back in a minute. He went to the admissions office to fill out the paperwork. He said he wanted to take care of everything."

"I have insurance."

"I know, hon. I told him. But he insisted. And you know how he is when he makes up his mind to something."

Do I ever, she thought to herself.

Bryon looked as though he wanted to add something more, but he didn't. Pausing, he gazed down at her. "I've already given Zac strict orders concerning your recovery. As soon as the cast is set, you can go home—but be sure to listen to what he says."

Great, Lainie thought grudgingly. Didn't Bryon have any idea what he'd done? The last thing she needed was to have Zachary dictating her life, even if it was just for a few measly days. Knowing him as she did, there was little doubt in her mind that he would take full advantage of the fact that she was at his mercy.

But then again, wouldn't that place him at her beck and call? Her mood perked up considerably.

Lainie was leaning back against the headboard, pillows propped behind her. She watched Zachary position the TV just right for her viewing.

"How's this?" he asked.

In the last hour she'd asked him to bring her knitting basket, the book she'd started a few days ago and now the television.

"That's fine."

He rose to his full height, placed his hands on his hips and took a long, deep breath. His emerald gaze fell on the small crystal bell he had placed on her nightstand after returning from the hospital. He'd told her to ring it when she needed him, and she had—several times. By now Lainie had no doubt that he would have liked nothing better than to smash it against the wall.

"Were you busy downstairs when I called you?" she asked, her dark eyes wide and innocent looking.

"Yeah, I guess you could say that."

"What were you doing?" she asked pleasantly. Too pleasantly.

He took another deep breath. "I was working on a couple of songs for a new album. Will you be needing anything else?"

She shrugged. "No, not that I can think of."

He gave her a fake smile. "I'm sure you'll think of something once I'm downstairs, so why not try to do it now, while I'm up here?"

"I can't seem to think of a single thing."

He worked his jaw for several seconds. Then he turned and strode out the door.

Lainie heard his heavy footsteps descending the stairs and smiled. Her demands were getting on his nerves, and she loved it. After all, she owed him. He'd had no right to kiss her the way he had this morning. Her mouth was still tender from it.

And so was her heart, she reminded herself.

Twenty minutes later she found she couldn't concentrate on anything. The television was a constant noise that she wasn't even listening to. Knitting was impossible, as was trying to read. She kept wondering why she was trying to find a reason to ring that little bell. Was it really to irritate Zachary, the way she told herself, or did she actually want his company, even if it was just for a brief moment?

Her heart pounded when realization dawned on her. What in the world was she going to do when he left—which she knew could be anytime. Surely he was tiring of the game he'd been playing with her. Did he have any idea what he'd done to her plain-Jane life, coming home like this? Did he know what he'd done to her heart?

If he did, he didn't care, she reminded herself. So she had to stop feeling guilty about lying to him.

Suddenly he was standing in her doorway, lifting one side of his mouth in a smile, his fingertips tucked in the front pockets of his jeans. For a split second her heart rolled over and died. "Need something?" he asked.

"I—I didn't ring the bell," she said in self-defense.

"I know," he answered with a self-conscious grin spreading across his handsome face. "I guess I'm just feeling guilty about losing my patience with you."

Was that an apology? To her?

She didn't know what to say. "I guess I'm not the best patient in the world. I hate being cooped up."

"Would you like to help out with the songs I'm working on?"

"Who, me? You can't be serious."

"Sure I am," he said with a grin.

"But how could I help?" She was afraid to think back to their youth. It could never be that way for them again.

He shrugged. "Who knows till you try?"

Watch him as he created his music? That seemed so intimate.

"Your ideas will be fresh." He cocked his head to one side. "What do you say?"

He sounded sincere, as if he really wanted her help, and his little-boy plea was enough to make her consider his request. They had shared some of their best times together working on his music. She didn't have the voice Zachary did, but she could carry a tune. And he was right about one thing; there had been a time when she had been good at putting words to his songs.

"Well, I guess I could give it a try—but I'm not promising anything," she added. "So don't be disappointed if nothing comes of this."

He nodded. "I'll get my guitar."

In no time at all she found herself laughing at her own combinations of words, often with Zachary's rich laughter joining her. But he praised her for her better efforts and encouraged her to continue. It was fun, relaxing—sometimes exciting—and they continued working until they put together a story about a young man saddened over the loss of his one true love.

For two hours they were lost in their efforts, giving and sharing with one another. Even to Lainie, who thought herself a pretty tough critic, the song sounded good by the time they finished. Add a five-man band behind him and she felt Zac might have himself another hit.

She smiled, pleased at the outcome of their time together, and equally pleased that Zachary seemed to like it, too.

"See. I told you you could help. You have to learn to trust me."

Lainie's smile widened. "It really does sound good, doesn't it?"

He grinned back. "Yeah, it does."

"It was fun."

"You're good at this, you know. You ought to think about doing it—even as a hobby." Standing and stretching his muscles, he added, "Maybe we can try it again sometime."

"I'd like that."

"I can just see it now," he drawled. "Number-one single of the week, written by Benjamin and Benjamin. Now that ought to raise a few eyebrows in Nashville," he said.

A bittersweet pain gripped her, but she remained in control and even forced a genuine-sounding laugh. "I'm afraid Nashville will have to wait. For now, a tub of hot water will do me just fine."

A slow, easy grin spread across his face. "How are you going to manage that with your cast?"

Lainie frowned. "I hadn't thought about it, but I'm sure I can manage."

"I guess you're going to need some help."

"I said I can manage."

"Oh for heaven's sake, let's not start that again," he said. "Remember what happened the last time?"

She didn't argue the point, and after deciding to wrap a towel around herself to keep from being completely exposed to his view, she allowed him to help her into the tub, her cast wrapped in a plastic bag and dangling over the edge. She prevented her thoughts from dwelling on the feel of his warm hands on her body. One thing, though, it was awfully hard to stay angry with someone who handled you as if you were made of porcelain.

Later, after a long soak, Lainie found herself losing at a game of Scrabble. Normally she was good at the game, and when Zachary had suggested that they play, she hadn't for one moment considered the possibility of losing. Now it was fast becoming a reality. Concentrating, she moved her letters from place to place on the small wooden pedestal in front of her, forming words.

After a while she asked, "Have you been practicing at this, too?"

Zac shook his head and smiled. "What's the matter? Is the English major having a hard time losing a game of Scrabble to a mere high school graduate?"

She gave him a bland look. "No, that's not why I asked."

He shrugged. "I happen to like the game and play as often as I can."

"Somehow I can't picture you as a Scrabble freak."

"There are a lot of things you don't know about me," he answered while placing a five-letter word on the board. Then he lifted his eyes to hers.

A hot rush ran through Lainie. She'd thought she knew all there was to know about him—but suddenly she needed to know more. Her hand trembled as she lifted the pencil. "Uhh...how many points is that?"

After winning the game, Zac requested her company downstairs while he prepared dinner. She was delighted to leave her room for whatever reason and gladly helped him peel the shrimp for the gumbo he insisted he could cook.

He played his part as a chef to the hilt, tying an apron around his waist and carefully calling out the name of each ingredient in French. Most of the words were nothing more than Cajun slang he'd learned as a child, but Lainie couldn't help but smile at his lighthearted gestures.

"Mon Dieu! C'est bon," he said after tasting the hearty Cajun soup. Using a blue porcelain ladle, he stirred the mixture of roux, water, seasonings and shrimp. "Want a taste?"

Lainie shook her head. "No, not yet. Have you added the okra?"

He gave her a temperamental frown, much like a small child would have done after being told by an adult to eat everything on his plate, including the mustard greens. "I don't like okra in gumbo."

"You don't have to put it in. It was just a suggestion."

"Good."

Gazing at her outstretched leg, Lainie said, "This cast is going to be a nuisance."

He glanced back. "You'll get used to it." Then, in almost the same breath, he added casually, "Oh, Lainie, by the way, I almost forgot to tell you."

"Tell me what?" she asked, taking a swallow from the glass of iced tea he'd fixed her. She was beginning to relax and enjoy herself. Maybe they could be friends.

"Alyse called while you were in the tub. I told her about your ankle, and she's driving in from Houston tonight."

"Tonight! She's coming here?" Lainie said. Forgetting her cast, she attempted to stand and nearly fell.

Zachary took three quick steps to her side, grabbed hold of her waist and helped her regain her balance before setting her back in the chair. "What's the matter with you?"

Unbridled panic seized her. Suddenly his hands, his entire person, seemed threatening. She pushed at him. "Don't touch me. Why didn't you tell me Alyse was coming?" she asked angrily.

"I just did."

"She must have called hours ago."

"Calm down. You're acting like I said the Russians are coming. It's just your daughter."

Lainie glanced around the room. "If she sees us like this, she's—she's bound to get the wrong idea."

"Just what could she possibly assume that would be the wrong idea?"

"You don't understand. I don't want her to think..."

"You don't want her to think what? That we were once lovers? She's not a child, Lainie."

"Look, I've sheltered Alyse. So did Cory. She doesn't know anything about us. Do you think I sat her down

one day and said, 'Now that you're old enough, I want
to tell you that I once had an affair with your famous
uncle'? It's not something a mother would brag about to
her own daughter.''

"It was before you and Cory got married. Like you
said, we were kids. It's not like we betrayed Cory. I
think—"

"It doesn't matter what you think!" Lainie yelled at
him. She could feel herself losing control. Tears threatened to spill from her eyes. She wanted to run from the
room, but she couldn't even walk. Zachary had been
carrying her everywhere. Where were her lousy crutches,
anyway?

Words she had never spoken aloud tumbled from her
lips. "We were kids, all right. And what we did meant
nothing. We just let ourselves get out of control like a lot
of teenagers do. There's no reason why Alyse needs to
know about that."

His eyes narrowed. "I'm not so sure that's true."

"Well, I am."

"We'll see about that."

"What do you mean?"

His grin was devilish. "If you want to make her sus-
picious of us, just keep acting this way."

"You could leave now, you know, before she gets
here."

"What? And miss your saintly performance? Not on
your life, baby. I bought a ticket, and I'm staying for the
entire play."

"Zachary, if you do anything that makes her suspi-
cious . . . I'll . . . I'll never forgive you!"

"Well, it'll be just one more grievance to add to your
list."

"Don't flatter yourself, Zachary. I don't give you that much thought."

He looked directly into her eyes, a cocky grin on his face. "I don't believe you."

"Think whatever you like."

"I happen to believe you still care."

"You're a fool if you think that!" she exclaimed.

"And you're a bigger one if you think I don't see through your little charade. Face it. You're not that good an actress."

His voice always took on a throaty quality when he was angry. And it always rattled Lainie down deep inside.

Zachary yanked open the door to the refrigerator, got himself a beer and slammed the door shut, rattling the glassware on top. He mumbled something under his breath. Lainie started to reply, then thought better of it. Besides, he was right about one thing. If Alyse noticed any animosity between them, she would surely question it, and in doing so, she just might decide to probe deeper into things Lainie didn't want to discuss with her daughter—ever.

Lainie took a deep breath to steady her nerves. "Alyse means the world to me. I'll do anything I have to in order to protect her. You had better understand that."

"Believe me, I understand more than you think."

If he was trying to frighten her with his insinuations, he was succeeding. "Zachary, surely you have something or—or someone in your life that means more to you than anything in the world, don't you?"

"I'm surprised you think I'm that human."

"Please—try to understand how I feel."

"Why don't you tell me how you feel? Go ahead," he said. "Explain to me what's it like being a parent, Lainie. I've never had that pleasure."

Leveling his gaze on her, he waited for her answer, but it never came, because a loud thud just beyond the back door drew their attention. Suddenly the door burst open, and a disheveled but smiling young brunette stepped inside.

"Hi!" she said enthusiastically. "I'm home!"

Chapter Eight

"Mama!" Alyse said. She was wearing a light aqua jogging suit with Who Cares? written in script across the front. She headed toward her mother, her white canvas shoes squeaking as she bounced across the distance separating them.

The long dark hair she'd inherited from her father was pulled into a ponytail at the top of her head and flopped around with a life of its own. In the privacy of their minds, both Zachary and Lainie thought her the epitome of youth and the living proof of the love they had once shared.

"Lyse!" Lainie exclaimed, hugging her daughter. "You didn't have to come all the way from Houston, for heaven's sake. I'm fine."

"I wanted to see for myself," Alyse replied, pulling away just enough to gaze at her mother. "You look sort of surprised to see me, though."

"That's because Zachary just thought to tell me you called earlier."

Lainie's gibe went undetected by her daughter, but Zachary was a hundred percent more perceptive. Lainie lifted her gaze to his, issuing a silent warning.

He read the message in her adamant glare. It did little to quell the mixed feelings he experienced while watching mother and daughter embrace. The love between them was obvious. The fact that he was an outsider looking in was even more obvious. It made a sick, lonely feeling settle in his chest and slide slowly down to the pit of his stomach. It was similar to the feeling he'd had when he found out Lainie had married his younger brother without so much as giving him a second thought.

Lainie saw the expression on Zac's face, and the guilt she'd tried to keep carefully contained all these years sprang a leak and oozed through her body like hot lava. Shaken by the unexpected emotion, she looked away.

Why should I feel guilty? she argued with herself. I did what I had to do to protect my child. Twenty years ago anyone in my predicament would have done the same thing. Zac made it quite clear that he didn't want to know anything about me much less the baby I was carrying. If I'd waited any longer I would have had to tell my parents, and they never would have survived the scandal. I did the right thing, the *only* thing.

Alyse studied her mother's thoughtful expression, then followed her outstretched leg, resting her eyes briefly on the white cast that started just below Lainie's knee. "I didn't interrupt anything, did I?"

"No—of course not," Lainie answered with a nervous laugh. "Why would you think such a thing?"

Alyse shrugged. "I don't know. I just . . . Oh, never mind. It's nothing."

"How was your trip?" Zac asked.

Alyse shrugged, blushing slightly under her famous uncle's steady gaze. "Oh, okay. Did you get my letter thanking you for the tickets you gave me?"

"No, honey, I haven't. Sometimes it takes a while for my mail to catch up with me. I'll make it a point to check on it the minute I get back."

"Oh," Alyse replied, disappointment in her voice.

"Say, Lyse," Lainie said, clearing her throat. "How did you manage to get time off from school—and your job?"

"I'm between semesters right now."

"Oh, right. I'd forgotten. But what about your job?"

Alyse dropped her eyes to the floor and appeared reluctant to answer. Finally she took a deep breath and said, "I don't work at the bookstore anymore, Mama. I'm working in a restaurant—as a singer. They're actually paying me to sing." She glanced from her mother to Zac, and when her eyes met his, she gave him a *please help me* look.

"A singer!" Lainie repeated. "What in the world has gotten into you? You can't work that late into the night and still have time for your studies." She blinked a couple of times. "I—I can't believe you did something like that." Then she glared in Zac's direction.

"Now, Mom, just listen," Alyse said, speaking almost as fast as an auctioneer. "I work Wednesdays, Fridays and every other Saturday night—but I'm off this weekend. I can make more money in those three nights than working every afternoon and some nights at the bookstore. And it's only one school night. It's a nice, respectable restaurant. Even you would approve."

"I can't believe it," Lainie repeated. "This is so out of character for you. I'd like to know who influenced you to do such a thing." Again she looked in Zac's direction.

"Nobody influenced me. I saw the ad in the newspaper and decided to take a chance. What's wrong with that?"

"How can you even ask such a question? You know your father wanted you to graduate from college."

"Daddy wanted the best for me. He never laid down a lot of ground rules like you did."

Lainie gasped. "Don't you think I want the best for you?"

"Of course, Mom," Alyse said, her voice trembling. "It's just that you get so uptight. With you, everything in life has to go in sequence, just like you've planned it, or not at all. Life doesn't always cooperate. Look at what happened to Daddy. Was that planned? Of course not, but we have to go on and learn to make the best of it."

"She's right, Lainie."

Lainie gathered every ounce of courage she had and glared at Zachary. "I can't see any reason for you to get involved in this discussion." Then she looked at her daughter. "We'll talk about this later."

"That's what you always say."

Standing off to the side, Zachary listened intently. Lainie was already angry because of his last remark. Lord knows she'd probably come unglued if he said any more on Alyse's behalf, although it was obvious his daughter needed help.

Lainie glanced from Alyse to Zachary. "She wants to be a star. Did you hear that? Tell her . . . tell her what it's really like out there."

"I'm not sure I should interfere. Maybe if the two of you sat down and discussed it—"

"What's there to discuss? Alyse is only nineteen years old. She should be spending all her spare time studying for her degree in accounting, not...not entertaining some fantasy of becoming a star." Turning once again to her daughter, Lainie asked, "Don't you know how much your father wanted you to get a good education?"

"Lainie, I don't think she intends to quit college."

"Nobody asked you."

Zachary's face lost all expression. "You're right. This is between the two of you." He turned with the intention of walking out of the room.

"No, Uncle Zachary. Please don't leave," Alyse pleaded. "Mother, there isn't any reason to take out your anger on him. He's only trying to help."

Was there no peace in this world? Lainie wondered. All she wanted to do was live out the rest of her life in the quiet solitude she'd become accustomed to in the past months. She'd made a safe, secure world where she wasn't forced to think about the past. It was a place where she didn't have to deal with anything more pressing than her students' final exams or the parish council meetings once a month. Why did she have to fight for the one ounce of sanity she had left since Zachary's reappearance in her life?

Carefully she observed the two people before her. She could tell by the set look in their near identical eyes that they had somehow sided together. She could almost have laughed at the irony of the situation, but she was afraid that if she started, she'd never stop. Alyse had wanted to be a singer for as long as Lainie could remember, telling everyone in town that she'd gotten her talent from her famous uncle. If only she'd known the truth.

"I'm going into the den," Lainie said quickly, feeling flushed. "We'll talk about this later—in private." As she stood to leave, Zac walked to her side and slipped his arm around her waist.

She looked him directly in the face. "I can walk by myself.

Determination lined his features. "I'll help you."

"I don't need any help."

"I insist."

She was immediately pressed against his lean body, and she remained against him as they headed, step by step, in the direction of the parlor. Because of their closeness, she was barely conscious of what her daughter was jabbering about behind them.

Alyse, much to Lainie's relief, didn't seem to pay any attention to the episode. She chatted on as she followed behind them as if nothing at all was out of the ordinary. "Now that we're finally getting to know each other," she said to Zac, "what can I call you? Uncle Zachary sounds so... old."

Zachary lowered Lainie into a chair and placed her foot on a stool. "Zac's fine with me."

Alyse bit her bottom lip in thoughtful consideration. "Zac," she repeated.

"Are you comfortable?" Zachary asked, placing his hands on his hips as he looked down at Lainie.

"I'm just fine," she replied.

Zachary's insides were shaking, and he had no idea why, unless it was because the three of them—father, mother, child—were all within touching distance of one another. A sudden, overwhelming urge to become a permanent part of their lives grew so incredibly strong within him that he felt nauseated. That wasn't part of his plan, either.

Alyse dropped onto the sofa. "Did Mama tell you how Daddy used to pull out the family albums when y'all were kids?'' she asked Zac. "We'd sit together on the floor, open several of them at one time and he'd tell me stories of when you and he were kids. Sometimes Mama would join us, but usually it was just Daddy and me...." Her voice drifted off. For a moment she seemed lost in her own thoughts; then suddenly she came back with a smile. "Do you think we could do that while you're here? I really miss those times."

"I'd like that, hon. We can do it any time you'd like."

"Alyse! That was a special time you shared with your father," Lainie replied quickly. "It wouldn't be the same."

"Nothing's the same now that Daddy's gone, Mama. But life goes on, and if there's one thing I learned from him, it was to go forward and make the most of each day—of what we have. He always wanted that for you and me." She looked at her mother with a sad smile on her face.

Clearing his throat, Zac exited. He returned moments later with Alyse's bags tucked under his arms. "I'll take these up. Why don't you sit with your mother while I finish dinner? It's been a trying day for her. I'll call when the food's done."

Alyse stretched out her legs, crossing them at the ankles, and clutched a throw pillow to her breast. "That's fine with me. I'm not much help in the kitchen, anyway. Suzy Homemaker I'm not. That's Mama's department."

Lainie glanced at a handwritten note near the telephone. She frowned. "I see Debra called while I was in the shower. Zachary must have forgotten to tell me that, too. I guess I'd better phone to see what she wanted."

She reached for the telephone on a nearby table. She lifted the receiver and was about to dial her friend's number when she heard someone speaking on the line.

"Mona, it's Zac. How're the plans for the benefit going? It's coming up pretty soon, you know."

"I know. Everything's in order."

After a moment Lainie laid the phone down, a hot flush rushing through her body. She hadn't intended to listen. It was something she'd never done. She glanced at her daughter, who, fortunately, had picked up a magazine and was thumbing through it, apparently unaware of the eavesdropping that had been committed just a few feet away.

Realizing he wasn't planning to be here much longer, Lainie vowed to keep up an even stronger guard.

"Gumbo's done," Zachary announced moments later from the kitchen doorway, bringing her out of her wayward thoughts.

Suddenly, without warning, he walked over and lifted her from the recliner.

"Put me down," she said anxiously. "I *can* walk, you know."

Zachary winked at Alyse, who was staring at them with a startled look on her face. She jumped up from the sofa as though to help, but instead fell in step behind them. Once they reached the kitchen, she quickly pulled out a chair for her mother.

Lainie gave Zac a hostile glare as she spoke to Alyse. "Your uncle has been acting like a fool today."

"Oh, Mom, I think he's charming," Alyse replied, admiration shining in her eyes. "Don't you?"

Over Alyse's dark head, two pairs of eyes sparred, one male and amusingly green, the other female and spitfire brown. "I suppose so," Lainie said, "if you like his type."

Zac raised his eyebrows. "And what type is that, may I ask?"

Choosing to ignore him completely, Lainie looked away.

Dinner was a strain for Lainie. Zac and Alyse, however, didn't seem to notice. The conversation between them flowed steadily.

"This is great, isn't it, Mom?" Alyse asked midway through the meal. "I only wish Daddy were here, too." She turned concerned eyes to Zachary. "He would have loved having you here."

Zachary's expression became serious. "I wish I'd taken the time to come home sooner. I always thought I would, but I never got around to it."

"It really is a shame," Alyse answered.

"Yeah," Zac replied. "I missed out on a lot of good years with my brother. I let everything else get in the way. There was either a concert"—*or your mother*—"or a new album"—*or simply too much raw pain*—"or an interview of some kind coming up. I'll always regret that I let all those things stand in the way of being with him. And now it's too late." He reached for her hand and covered it with his. "It's very important to me that we become friends, Alyse."

Awed by his confession, Alyse smiled at him. "I'd like that very much. I've always been so curious about you."

One corner of Zac's mouth lifted in a smile.

Alyse glanced at her mother and was surprised to find her as white as the paper napkin in her lap. "What's wrong, Mama?"

Lainie shook her head, hoping neither of them could see how tense she actually was. She was trying to tell

herself that it was probably only natural for the two of
them to want to get to know each other. It was just
harmless curiosity on their part and didn't mean a thing.
At least, not as long as they didn't discover the truth. As
Zachary had just said, what they'd missed in the past
couldn't be made up.

So why did she have to keep arguing that issue over and
over with herself?

"Can I get you anything, Lainie?" Zac asked, the deep
timbre of his voice forcing her from her thoughts.

"Huh? No, I'm fine. Since it's obvious your life has
been extremely busy, when did you find time to become
a chef?"

He laughed. "I'm no chef, believe me. Gumbo and
chocolate chip cookies are as far as my cooking skills go.
I can, however, whip up just about any cocktail you've
ever heard of." His grin broadened, and it looked so
scrumptious to her that she decided it could have been
dessert.

"Did you ever tend bar?" Alyse asked enthusiastically.

"Didn't have much choice. That's how I made my living for a while. Most entertainers usually become a master at some other trade while waiting to make it big. I
certainly was no different." He glanced at Alyse. "It's
not easy, honey, if that's what you think. I want you to
remember that if ever you decide to pursue the dream I
see shining in your eyes. It'll take everything you have to
give—and a whole lot more. Just be sure in your heart
that it's worth the sacrifice."

"Oh, I know it would be," Alyse said dreamily. "You
don't regret your life, do you?"

Lainie held her breath while waiting for his answer.

Zachary gazed across the table at Alyse. "For the most part, no. But there are a few things I'd change if I could."

"Like what?" Alyse asked innocently.

"Alyse!" Lainie exclaimed. "That's enough. You shouldn't pry into your uncle's personal life. It's none of our business."

Alyse blushed. "I'm sorry," she replied quickly. "I didn't mean to pry."

"No apology needed. I don't consider your questions prying. Ask me anything you'd like," he said, the tone of his voice making his point clear to Lainie.

Taking advantage, Alyse asked, "Well...just what would you do differently if you could?"

"Ohhh...I guess my biggest regret is not being able to lead a normal life. I'm almost forty years old, and I've never slowed down enough to stay in one place for very long. This house is the only home I've ever known." Suddenly thoughtful, he glanced from Lainie to Alyse.

Alyse smiled. "All these years I've known you were my uncle, but I could never really identify with you being family. It just didn't seem real to me. I'm really happy that's going to change from now on."

Zachary glanced over to Lainie, who had laid her spoon down. "How about you, Lainie? How do you feel about all this?"

She stared at him for several seconds without answering. Then, looking down at her bowl, she said, "I don't have an opinion one way or the other."

"That's not answering my question."

"Oh, don't mind Mama, Zac," Alyse said, clearly wanting to avoid a disagreement between them. "She always feels it's her duty to be serious. Daddy was the only one who could make her laugh. Right, Mom?"

Lainie turned her gaze in her daughter's direction. "Does it matter what I think?"

Alyse rolled her eyes, then looked at Zachary and shrugged. "See what I mean?"

By the time the gumbo bowls were removed and dessert was served, one thing was obvious to Lainie. Alyse thought the world of Zac, and it showed. Much to Lainie's distress, they seemed completely relaxed in each other's company. Worry made her glance from one pair of green eyes to the other. Father and daughter were so very much alike. The smile Zac wore was lazy and knowing, the smile on Alyse's face bright and innocent, but they had the same slant, the same earth-rocking appeal that made them so much the special people they were destined to be. Her heart cried out at the injustice that life had handed her. When she glanced once again at Zachary, he looked in her direction and stared for a moment. From the intensity of his gaze, she wondered if he could read her thoughts. She was the first to look away.

There had been times over the years when she had been weak and had wanted Zachary to still love her like he'd promised. But then she would think of Cory and the unselfish way he'd helped her. She would suffer from guilt for days, reminding herself that she'd made a choice when she'd married Cory, and it was a choice she would never go back on. And she hadn't. No matter how sad she'd become, no matter how much she'd needed Zachary, she'd never lost track of what Cory meant to her. So what if she was having a hard time handling the lie she'd told? She'd lived with guilt most of her life, and she could continue to do so forever, if necessary.

And it *was* necessary.

"I think I'll call it a night. How about you, Lyse?" Lainie asked, stifling a deliberate yawn.

"Ohhh...I don't know. I'd rather stay up awhile longer and talk with Zac—unless he's going to bed, too." She glanced toward her uncle and smiled. "There are so many things I want to know about you. I'd like to hear all about the early years of your career—and about all the attention you receive now. It looks so glamorous."

Zac threw his head back and laughed. The sound, as thick and rich as south Louisiana coffee, rumbled deep inside his chest. "I hate to burst your bubble, little darling, but my life has been far from glamorous. You sound like your mother. Do the two of you read the same gossip columns?"

Alyse gave her mother a questioning look, but it was Zac who answered it.

"It's just a private joke. Forget it." Glancing at Lainie, he said, "I'll help you to bed."

"I can manage by myself."

"Oh, sure you can. You can hobble up a flight of stairs on one good leg while Alyse and I ignore you.... Come off it, Lainie. You need help, and you know it."

"Really, Mama, you can't possibly climb those stairs alone. What's gotten into you?"

"I think it's time you both realized I'm not an invalid. By tomorrow I'll be an old pro at this," Lainie replied.

"That's tomorrow," Zac said lazily. "But tonight you're still my patient, and I'll carry you to bed, so just relax and enjoy it. Try to picture me as Prince Charming."

He winked at Alyse.

"This could get interesting," she chimed in with a broad smile on her face.

Prince Charming indeed, Lainie thought. The devil would be more like it. And he'd said to relax. What an insane idea. How was she supposed to do that when her nerves were already strung so tight that her blood was having trouble flowing through her veins?

Not one single word was exchanged between them as Zachary, exerting little effort, started up the stairs with her in his arms. Lainie encircled his neck with her arm and then glanced back just in time to see a strange look come over her daughter's face as she watched the two of them climb the stairs. But Alyse turned away abruptly and went back into the kitchen before Lainie could say anything to her.

The bedside lamp in Lainie's room cast an alluring glow. After setting her on the edge of the bed, Zachary drew back the sheet and began fluffing up her pillows.

Hearing the rustling sound as he smoothed out the wrinkles in the bedding was almost more than she could handle at the moment. "Thank you. That's fine. You can go back downstairs and proceed to charm Alyse."

Zac stepped back, his expression a mass of contradicting emotions as he allowed his silky gaze to rest on the soft fullness of her breasts. It lingered there momentarily before sliding to her face.

"Lainie, I'm getting pretty tired of your constant sarcasm. Since I've come home, I've tried all sorts of different tactics with you. I've even changed my mind about a few things I never thought I would. But nothing I do changes your attitude toward me. I'm not the monster you seem to think I am."

"Don't try to play games with me, Zachary. I've been that route with you before. It didn't get me anywhere the last time, and I'm not stupid enough to think it will now."

"Okay," he said, his jaw clenched tight. "If this is how you want it, then so be it. But first I want you to answer one question for me."

Lainie felt as though she were smothering. She didn't want to hear what this one question could be. Not tonight. Not ever. "I can't imagine what you could have to ask me," she said nervously.

"It's about what happened in the past—between you and me and—"

"Let's just forget about the past. It has nothing to do with today."

His emerald gaze narrowed. "You'd like that, wouldn't you?"

Lainie glared at him. "Yes."

Suddenly he grabbed her by the arm. "Well, not this time, babe. This time I want some answers from you. Alyse—"

"Leave my daughter out of this. She has nothing to do with this."

Zac's temper flared. "She has everything to do with this. She represents everything you've lied to me about."

Dumbfounded, Lainie stared up at him. "Nooo..."

He tightened his grip on her arm. "I want the truth, damn you. *Does* she have everything to do with us?"

"Nooo..." Lainie whispered, shaking her head emphatically. "No...she has nothing to do with us."

"You're lying, Lainie," he said, his jaw tightening. "And if I had any sense at all, I'd hate you for lying to me like you've done, and so help me, at the moment I do. She's mine, isn't she? Alyse is my daughter. Mine and yours. Say it, Lainie." Desperate to have her say the words he wanted—needed—to hear, he grabbed her chin and lifted her face. "Look me in the eyes and say it, damn you."

"Yes," she said, feeling faint, as if someone had just slashed open every vein in her body, draining her of life. She wanted to tell him how much she hated him for what he was doing to her—and to Alyse, too. But she couldn't utter another sound. She couldn't even think clearly any longer. There was a humming in her ears.

Zachary saw the empty look on her face. Damn his temper. He'd gone and lost it again, and now look at the mess he'd made of things.

Why be upset? his inner voice asked. Wasn't this part of the plan? Weren't you going to stick the knife into her heart at just the right time? Well, partner, looks like you've succeeded.

Just shut the hell up, he warned the nagging voice.

Voices drifted in from the darkness. Gradually the room became lighter. Lainie groaned out her momentary lack of understanding as the blue-flowered wallpaper in her bedroom stopped swimming before her eyes and settled down to resemble the pattern she remembered. Slowly her eyes shifted to the left and met others that stared down at her in silence. A mouth, frowning in concern, became the center of her attention as lips moved and words came out. Words that slowly penetrated her dazed mind.

"How do you feel, Lainie?"

It was a familiar voice, but still the fog in her head hadn't lifted enough for her to identify it. "I...I don't know."

"Don't be scared. You just fainted. In a few minutes you'll be fine."

"Cory?" Lainie asked.

"No, Lainie. It's Zachary. Cory's...not here."

"He's in the hospital, isn't he? I need to go to him. He needs me," she replied anxiously, sitting up despite the pressure of strong hands on her shoulders.

"No," a sad voice replied as those firm but gentle hands lowered her back into the warmth of her bed. "Cory's not in the hospital."

Lainie heard muffled crying in the distance. "What's wrong? Is he worse? Where's Alyse? Don't let her see him...hear him.... She'll be frightened.... He says things she shouldn't hear—things she won't understand.... Please...someone find her. Don't..."

"It's okay," the deep throaty voice said over and over, its soothing monotone a comfort in her disoriented state. "Everything is okay. Don't fight. Just relax...that's right. Close your eyes and just relax."

"What do you think, Bryon?" Zachary asked wearily forty-five minutes later, his voice filled with guilt. Thank God Bryon had arrived to look at Lainie.

"She seems to be suffering from a form of hysterical amnesia, where a person refuses to recall something they can't handle." He shook his head. "From what you've just told me, it probably has something to do with whatever the two of you were talking about before she fainted."

"My God.... Will she be all right?" Zachary asked, running his fingers through the dark hair hanging down his forehead. "What can we do to help her?"

"In most cases a person usually gets over something like this without much outside help. She might recall everything when she wakes up in the morning. But then again, it could be days, even weeks, before she allows herself to remember. It could come in bits and pieces—or it could come back all at once. About the only thing we can do at the moment is wait. If her memory doesn't return, then we'll need to consider treatment."

"What kind of treatment?"

"Hypnosis, or possibly medication."

"How can she just forget part of her life like that?"

"She hasn't forgotten, Zac. You have to understand the human mind. She's refusing to acknowledge a very stressful situation."

"I feel like such a jerk. If I hadn't lost my temper, she'd be fine now."

"I'm not so sure. This was probably inevitable. I think Lainie has always felt guilty about the relationship between you and her and Cory. Cory seemed to accept things as they were and even tried to help her deal with her own feelings, but inside, I don't think she ever did. Lainie is really a strong person—maybe so much so that this is her only way of coping with things that she can't control any longer. It hasn't been that long since Cory's death, and with you coming back like this . . . well . . . I think it's been too much for her to handle."

"Just tell me she's going to be all right."

"There are never any guarantees, Zac—you know that. But I think so. More likely than not she'll be fine in a few days. We'll just have to watch her closely."

Zachary leaned his head back and stared at the ceiling for a long time. "What am I going to tell Alyse?"

"Why ask me? Aren't you the one who came home with all the answers?"

Zachary looked at his cousin. "You don't think I should have come back, do you?"

"Not for the reasons you say you did. Look, I'm not saying Lainie did the right thing by hiding the truth from you, but to come back for some personal vendetta, well, that's something else. Haven't both of you suffered enough? And what about Alyse? She's caught right in the middle."

"So you think I should just leave without telling her that I'm her father. Well, to be perfectly frank, I don't think that's quite fair, either."

"I'm not saying she shouldn't know. But not like this. Not as a means for revenge." Bryon looked Zachary in the face. "Do you really think you'll find peace if you do something as cruel as that? If so, you're not the same person you once were."

Zachary stared back. Tears glistened in his eyes, and he had to swallow back the need to release the painful emotions raging in him. He quickly glanced away.

"Have you stopped to consider the possibility that maybe you're angry with Lainie because you're still in love with her?"

Zachary walked to the kitchen window and stared down the long driveway.

Bryon cleared his throat. "I think before you continue trying to even the score with her, you need to stop and really think about what you want. You just might be surprised." He shook his head as he went on. "I don't envy you, my friend." He walked over to Zac and clasped his shoulder. "Maybe it's time you gave her the benefit of the doubt. Listen to her side of things."

"That won't help."

"How do you know? Look, I'm just saying that there are always two sides to a story. Maybe listening to what she has to say would put an end to this whole mess."

"It's too late for that," Zachary said, still staring out the window.

Sighing, Bryon walked to the door. "Well, there's nothing more I can do at the moment. If you need me, I'll be at home."

"Thanks, Bryon—for everything," Zac said. "I know it doesn't sound like much, but for a guy who has thousands of fans, all I really need right now is a friend."

"Has Alyse gone to bed?"

"Yes."

"Try to get some rest, too. You haven't been looking so hot these past few days."

After Bryon left, Zachary went up to his room and tried to sleep, but for the most part, it was useless. He finally drifted off somewhere around sunrise.

He was awakened when Alyse knocked on his door and announced she had biscuits and coffee waiting in the kitchen.

He dressed, then looked in on Lainie before heading downstairs. Finding her still asleep, he followed the smell of freshly brewed coffee.

Somewhere in the wee hours of the morning, he'd realized he no longer had the desire for revenge. There was nothing more for him here, and it was time he left.

What surprised him about that decision was that he found he really didn't want to go. He would have liked nothing better than to stay here with Lainie, loving her and getting to know his daughter as only a father could know his child. But that was impossible now. Lainie would never believe him after last night, and he really couldn't blame her. And as far as his daughter was concerned, at the moment he didn't feel he deserved to be called her father.

He simply needed to move on. Just like he'd always done. Another town, another concert, and in a few months this huge, empty void inside him would become a natural way of feeling. He wouldn't think about Lainie or Alyse so much. He wouldn't think of the dream he'd once had. He would force himself to think of tomorrow and the empty days to follow. He was tough, as tough as a man could be when it came to hiding a broken heart. He'd done it for years now.

He had to get a grip on his life. There were a lot of people in Nashville depending on him, and he couldn't let them down. Once he found someone qualified to care for Lainie while she recuperated, someone she could depend on—because Lord knew, she couldn't depend on him— he would be heading back to Nashville and out of her life.

He'd sure made a mess of things, and the losses he'd suffered weighed heavily on his heart.

The ironic part was that, like a fool, on the day he arrived in Harrington, he'd thought he had nothing to lose.

Chapter Nine

When he entered the kitchen, Zachary forced a smile. "Good morning," he said, not wanting to startle Alyse, whose back was to him.

She whirled around. "Good morning." Then, in almost the same breath, she asked, "Did you happen to check on Mama before coming down?"

"Yeah. She's still asleep."

"Yeah," she said anxiously. "She was sleeping when I looked in, too." Dressed in cutoff denim shorts and an overly large yellow T-shirt, she looked younger than her nineteen years.

She glanced back to the round tin pan on the top of the stove. "How about some biscuits?"

"Sure," Zac said, strolling across the floor as he rolled up the sleeves of his shirt. He poured himself a cup of coffee and picked up two biscuits before sitting down at the table. Alyse sat across from him.

"These might not taste worth a darn. I'm not a very good cook. I used Mama's recipe, but I'm sure I messed up somewhere along the line."

"Don't sell yourself short. Your mama's had a lot more practice."

"But she likes to cook. I'm not that crazy about it."

"Ohhh ... I see," Zac said, smiling as he slapped Lainie's homemade preserves inside his biscuits. "I guess you'd rather be standing on stage singing your heart out instead of slaving over a hot stove, huh?"

"Yeah," she said softly. "Something like that."

The next seconds were filled with silent uneasiness. Alyse reached over and touched the leaf of an English ivy sitting in a clay pot on a nearby windowsill. "I wonder if Mama's plants need watering," she said absently.

"You got me. The plants in my apartment would die if my housekeeper didn't take care of them," Zac replied.

And so time continued to drum by. Finally, with only a fraction of a second separating them, they both decided to speak.

"What did you say to Ma—"

"Alyse, I need to talk to you about—"

"You and Mama," Alyse finished for him after he stopped speaking in midsentence.

"Yeah," he said, feeling his heart swell to enormous proportions, almost smothering him. He hesitated, laying the knife he held on the edge of his plate and looking into her large, lucid green eyes that were so much like his own. "It's something that happened a long time ago— before she married Cory." He felt as if he were stammering like a nervous kid.

For crying out loud, Benjamin, he chastised himself, get a grip on yourself.

Alyse sat up straight, as though bracing herself. "Go on."

Zac took a deep breath and chose his next words carefully. "I realize you were never told that your mother and I...well...we were once in love. I guess your mother felt it wasn't something she could share with you."

When Alyse didn't speak, he took another breath and continued. "I loved her very much, more than I even realized when I first left home. It wasn't until I heard she'd married my brother that I realized just how much."

Alyse shook her head. "So that's why you never came back. It really had nothing to do with your career, did it?"

"No," Zac replied, shaking his head. "My career was just an easy excuse, something I could use without anyone questioning it."

"I see," Alyse said, sounding hurt that he'd lied to her. To all of them.

He reached out to touch her cheek. "Honey, I really don't think you do."

She turned her face from him. "So why did she marry my dad?"

Zac got up, ignoring the trembling in his legs and walked to the counter to pour himself another cup of coffee. Here was the one chance, the one moment he'd hoped to have with his daughter, and what was he going to do with it? Nothing...absolutely nothing at all. He wasn't going to tell her the truth. Not now, when she looked so vulnerable. If ever she was going to learn about him, it was going to be at the right time, for the right reason and from the right person—her mother. "I guess she decided she didn't want to be a part of the life I'd chosen."

Alyse looked at him for the longest time. "Are you trying to say that my mother is...is sick because she can't cope with me finding out the two of you once dated? Come on, I know my mother better than that. She's not a wimp."

Zac had to smile to himself at her choice words. "I wasn't implying that she is. I'm only saying she and I had a very complicated relationship that ended as soon as I left Harrington. The first thing I knew she was married to my brother, and I was left out in the cold. To be honest, I was downright angry about it for a long time."

"With all the other girls you could've had over the years, you must have loved her very much to feel that way."

Zac stared out the kitchen window, his face empty of emotion. "Yeah, I guess I did." He glanced down at his coffee cup before taking another swallow. "It was a long time ago."

"And now? Why did you come back after all this time? Is it because of Mama?"

His lips lifted in a sad, lopsided smile. "Let's just say I've learned some hard lessons since I've returned."

"She doesn't want you here, does she?"

"That's putting it mildly," he said.

"Did you ask her why she married Daddy like she did?"

Zac wondered why he was being put through hell this way. Not that he didn't in some ways deserve it, but the torment he felt at the moment couldn't have been worse if the devil himself had been the one questioning him.

"She and Cory were good friends long before she and I met."

Alyse didn't answer.

Zac had always felt that every man had a breaking point, but until now he'd never reached his, not even at the worst times in his life. But suddenly he felt as if the unwanted moment was fast approaching.

He stared out the window for several long moments. Once he felt under control, he glanced at Alyse and found her watching him.

"We look alike, don't we?" she said, turning her gaze out the window, then glancing back in his direction. Innocent emerald eyes met knowing ones.

"Yeah. We both look like my mother," he said, reminding her. "Your grandmother."

"I used to wonder about that as a kid. When I'd ask Mama about it, she would always explain to me about heredity and genes and all that stuff. She'd never just give me a straight answer." She looked Zac in the face. "Can you?"

As hard as it was, he stood his ground without flinching. "Nothing simpler than heredity and genes and all that stuff," he replied, hoping to make light of the moment. But he felt anything but light.

"What did you and my dad talk about when you got to the hospital? Did you make up?"

"Sort of," Zac replied, not wanting to tell her it had been too late to talk to Cory by the time he'd arrived. She already looked sad enough as it was. But Cory had been too sedated to make any sense of the words spoken to him or the words he spoke. His brother had only rambled incoherently without realizing what he said or who was listening.

She was quiet for several long moments, then suddenly she rose. "I'd better see if Mama's awake," she said, and in that instant, Zachary knew she wasn't really ready to hear the truth from him, or anyone, for that matter. At least, not yet. But he had a feeling the time was near when she would be. She was too much like him to ever settle for less than the truth.

"That's a good idea. I'll make another pot of coffee while you do."

Her sad smile left a bittersweet dent in his heart as she scooted out of the kitchen and up the stairs. Taking a deep breath, Zachary placed his dirty breakfast dishes in the sink and allowed his brain to sort through the tormented conversation of moments ago.

The past hung around him like a dense fog, reminding him that no one had a lifetime guarantee of happiness. As a matter of fact, nothing in life had a guarantee—not happiness, not love, not fame and fortune.

A few years ago he'd been able to convince himself that his career would eventually satisfy the hunger that still ate at him. For a while he'd even fooled himself into thinking he was over Lainie. But his career hadn't stopped the loneliness that overcame him each time a concert was over and the lights went out, sending his screaming fans home to their families. God, how he'd envied them. He had no one waiting for him—at least, not anyone who loved him the way he needed, the way Lainie once had. Oh, he had friends and co-workers who cared about him. But what he'd wanted was someone anxiously awaiting his return—someone besides the screaming groupies who followed stars from place to place, begging for attention in any way they could get it. He'd wanted someone to listen to his problems, someone who would want to make love with him in the middle of the night simply because she needed him more than life itself—and not his superstar image, but the man he really was. Sighing, he sat down and stared out the window, wondering how his life could have gotten so messed up when his young dreams had been so special.

About ten minutes later, Alyse came back down. "Mama's awake, but she's not very talkative. I told her I'd bring up a good breakfast, but she only wants coffee," she said, walking toward the cabinet.

"Is she any better?" Zac asked, concern gathering in his eyes.

"I—I don't know. I couldn't tell by what she said, and I was afraid to ask. I didn't want to upset her again."

"No," Zac replied. "Neither would I." He hesitated, then plunged ahead. "Look, I've been thinking.... I've got to get back to Nashville soon, and I've decided it's no use postponing it any longer. I've got a big benefit concert coming up in a couple of weeks. Originally I'd planned on staying another few days, but I don't think that's such a good idea now. I was wondering what you would think of hiring a nurse to care for your mother until she's better."

"I'll be here to do that."

"But even you can't stay that long. You've got a new job to worry about—and won't the summer semester start up soon?"

A speculative expression crossed her face. "That's true. But how long do you think it'll take for Mom to recover?"

"Total recovery? I don't know. Weeks, I would imagine, 'til that cast comes off." He refused to acknowledge the possibility that her amnesia might be the bigger problem.

"Well..." she said, biting her lower lip. "Maybe that's not such a bad idea. She'll need someone—although I'm sure she won't agree with that."

"I hadn't planned on asking what she thought. I was just going to do it."

Alyse smiled—really smiled—for the first time since the night before. "Well, you'd better be ready for a good old-fashioned tongue lashing."

"I know. That's why I want someone who can take charge . . . someone like Nurse Bell. Do you know her?"

Her grin widened. "Sure. Everyone in Harrington knows Nurse Bell. Oh, Zac, she'd be perfect."

"The only thing is, she works at the hospital."

"Yeah, but I think it's only part-time. Why don't you call Bryon? He'd know for sure."

By noon Zac had completed the arrangements for Lainie's care with Joanna Bell. Thanks to his cousin's input, she was more than willing to help out during her time off from the hospital. It was her duty, she had said, to help wherever she was needed.

During the morning Alyse had told him she thought her mother was doing better, but Zac knew he needed to see for himself, to be sure Lainie was all right, but in some odd way, he dreaded the encounter. What would she say when she saw him? Did she even recall their argument of the night before?

He walked upstairs and for a few moments just stood at Lainie's bedroom door, wondering what lay beyond. Finally he knocked lightly and entered at her reply.

His eyes automatically sought her in the bed and he was surprised to find she wasn't there. In almost the same instant he realized she was seated in a rocker near the window, wrapped in her blue silk robe, her foot propped up on a stool. Her hair had been brushed and pulled together at the nape of her neck, a ribbon holding it in place. Her cheeks were blushed a light pink, her lips a dewy rose. She looked lovely—vulnerable—and from the sadness that veiled her eyes, deeply hurt. Was Bryon right? Were there two sides to this awful mess?

"Hi," he said, hoping he sounded normal.

"Hi," she replied.

"How are you feeling?"

"Better . . . much better."

Unconsciously, he released the breath he'd held since entering. "That's good."

She attempted a smile, then turned and gazed back out the window. "It's a nice day, isn't it?"

"Yeah, it sure is."

"How warm is it outside?"

"The weatherman on the radio said the high today would be around eighty-six. It must be near that now."

She nodded, seemingly satisfied with his answer.

Small talk. They were making small talk like two strangers in an elevator.

"Lainie—"

"Zac—"

"You go ahead," they continued together, which finally forced a small smile from both of them.

Zachary looked around for a place to sit. "I'll be back in a second," he said, heading for his bedroom. He came back with a desk chair that he straddled near Lainie.

The moments that followed were quiet. Too quiet. Zachary felt a storm brewing inside her and waited for the first gale.

It never came.

Trying to relax, he folded his arms across the back of the chair and rested his chin on them, studying her at an angle. Was her memory still missing?

"Cory loved days like this," she said softly.

"Yeah, I remember."

"I miss him. I'll always miss him."

"I know."

She took a deep breath. "How long have you known?"

Known? He could have asked about what, but that wasn't necessary. He knew what she meant. "Since I saw him in the hospital. He was talking out of his head, but I understood most of it."

She looked so calm as she glanced his way that it alarmed him.

"I see," she said.

Tears gathered in her eyes. Laying her head on the back of the chair, she squeezed her eyes closed. A single tear trickled down her face, and Zac felt his heart constrict.

She let out her breath in a sigh. "So in the end, he unknowingly told our secret."

"Is that how you see it?" Zac asked.

"We'd made a promise—"

"Which he kept for twenty years," he said, cutting her off. "Twenty years, Lainie. That's a long time for someone to keep a secret like that—especially from his only brother. Don't you think he might have felt just a little guilty?"

Her eyes flew open and met his briefly. Then she turned to stare out the window. Cory? Guilty? He'd had no reason to feel guilty.

But maybe he had felt that way. Maybe he just hadn't told her.

Not once since his death had she considered such a possibility. But now...

Still, it didn't change anything between her and Zachary. Twenty years ago he had knowingly rejected her. And just a few days ago he'd lied to her. He'd said he'd come home for a rest, when all he'd really wanted was to destroy her world. Well, he'd succeeded.

Was Alyse going to be his next target?

"So what are you going to do now?"

"I'm leaving in the morning."

She jerked her startled gaze back to him. "Leaving?"

"Yes. I'm needed in Nashville."

"What about Alyse?"

He searched her face. "What about her?"

"What have you told her?"

"Nothing."

She looked baffled. "Do you plan to?"

"Not anymore."

She breathed a sigh of relief. "Oh, thank God."

"It's up to you now."

"What? You expect me to tell her the truth? You can't possibly believe I'd do such a thing."

His gut twisted in a knot. "I sure as hell do."

"You're crazy."

"You can't continue to cheat her out of the truth. She has a right to know who her father really is. If you *don't* tell her, then I *will*."

"You're doing this to hurt me, aren't you? Why?"

A sudden, uncontrollable anger seized him. He stood and shoved the chair from him. "Why? You have the nerve to ask me why? Well, I'll give you a reason why. You stole twenty years of my life from me."

She gaped at him. Confusion...pain...sorrow... they were all written across her face. "How can you stand there and say that?"

His eyes narrowed. "Are you really that unfeeling?"

The air rushed from her lungs. "How can you have the audacity to stand here and say something like that after all you put me through?"

He leaned down into her face. "What on earth is that supposed to mean?"

"You know perfectly well what that's supposed to mean. Don't stand there looking at me like—like you're all innocent," she stated.

"What are you talking about? I *am* innocent. True, I didn't think about the possibility of your getting pregnant when I left. I'll take the blame for that. But for God's sake, I was nineteen—and as green as grass. If I'd had any inkling that you were pregnant, I would gladly have come back to marry you. All you had to do was pick up the telephone."

Lainie exploded in anger. "Pick up the telephone?" she repeated. "Just how stupid do you think I am? I *did* phone you. For two weeks. You never returned one message I left."

"And just what kind of a fool do you think I am? You never called me—because if you had," he said, ramming the tip of his finger against his chest, "*I* would have been your husband for the last twenty years—not my brother."

Rage suffused Lainie's face with color. "I called you every day—sometimes twice a day—for two weeks. I left messages everywhere." Her voice was near hysteria. "Your manager finally returned my calls because you didn't even care enough to do it."

"My manager?"

"That's right, your manager. He told he how he was trying to get you to accept your responsibility, but you wouldn't listen. He said the only thing you wanted was to become a star. Finally he told me how sorry he was that you didn't want to have anything to do with me or the baby."

"That's a lie!" Zac yelled.

Lainie was so caught up in the moment that she ignored him and spoke louder. "He felt so sorry for me that he offered me money from his own pocket. He even tried to convince me that he had the connections to get me an abortion—which he said he'd pay for.'' Her mouth began to tremble. ''I couldn't stand the pity I heard in his voice. It ate at me until I finally called him back a couple of days later and said I'd made a mistake—that I wasn't pregnant after all. I told him to be sure to tell you. He promised he would. The next day Cory and I decided to get married.''

Zachary tried to absorb everything she was saying, but he couldn't. First of all, she wasn't making any sense. Bobby Jones had been his manager and a close friend from the very beginning of his career. The man wouldn't have done something like that behind his back. Not Bobby. He could be trusted. Zac *had* trusted him—for years.

If Lainie was telling the truth—and only if—why hadn't Bobby given him her messages?

Suddenly words his manager had spoken long ago came to mind. *''You're gonna be a superstar someday, and we can't let anything stand in your way.''* Had Bobby seen Lainie as a threat to his success?

No, that couldn't be it, he told himself, shaking his head to clear it. The man had seen the way he'd suffered over losing her. She was just trying to cover her lies.

''I think you're lying.''

''I don't care what you think anymore. I don't need you. As a matter of fact, I never needed you.''

''Is that so? Well, let's just see if that's true.''

Before she could react, his large, powerful hands grabbed her shoulders and his lips came down on hers in an all-consuming kiss.

She pushed hard on his wide shoulders, but he remained as unmoving as stone.

Slowly his kiss deepened, and she felt a need deep within him that she couldn't ignore. His hands slipped around her, and he pressed her body to his.

The passion they had held prisoner for so many years escaped, and for one wild, timeless moment, they abandoned everything but their undying need for each other.

The unexpected moment was so powerful that neither one of them could pull away. Not even the abrupt sound of a slamming door could shatter the moment.

Debra Cohen's voice rang through the house. "Hello? Where is everyone?"

Breathing hard, Zachary released Lainie and stared into her eyes.

Lainie touched her fingertips to her throbbing lips. Her body begged for the feel of his body.

Without flinching, he stepped away from her and said, "I'm going to get to the bottom of this if it's the last thing I do." Then he turned and walked away.

Chapter Ten

Packed and ready to leave first thing in the morning, Zachary lay across his bed, his hands folded behind his head, staring at the ceiling. The words he and Lainie had exchanged kept coming back to him. How could she have said those things? Didn't she know he could prove she was lying?

She'd sounded so sincere, as if everything she was saying was coming from her soul, but then, hadn't she sounded just as sincere years ago, when she'd said she would always love him? Could she really be as innocent as she claimed?

Was it possible that Bobby was the real culprit after all?

Suddenly he couldn't stand the anxiety any longer. Rising, he hurriedly dressed in jeans, a T-shirt and his favorite pair of old boots. Noiselessly, he carried his bags to his car, then came back inside to write a letter to Lainie, explaining his intentions. He placed the envelope on the table next to the bed, knowing Nurse Bell would find it and leave it for Lainie. Then he awakened Alyse.

She responded with a groan.

"Something's come up in Nashville and I need to see about it right away." Not sure if she understood him, he shook her again. "Alyse, do you hear me?"

"Uh-huh," she answered without opening her eyes.

"If either you or your mother needs anything, call me at this number," he said, scribbling something on a pad and placing it by her bed. "These people are good friends of mine. They'll know how to get in touch with me."

"Okay," Alyse said, dazed, though somehow managing to hug him in the process. It took every ounce of courage he had to turn and walk away.

Before long his Jaguar was careening toward Nashville, Tennessee. His purpose: to get to the truth, once and for all.

Someone jerked back the bedroom curtains, and sunlight streamed through the window near Lainie's bed. Her eyes sprang open.

"Good morning, Lainie," Nurse Bell said cheerfully. "I didn't want to awaken you earlier, but I think it's time now. Your daughter just left for nine-thirty Mass."

Lainie stared at the sparkling white nurse's uniform and cap. She frowned. "What are you doing here?"

"Well . . . my Lord. Didn't Zachary tell you he'd hired me to care for you until you were feeling better?"

Shaking her head in confusion, Lainie said, "No...he didn't tell me anything."

"Well, maybe he didn't get the chance. Alyse said he had to leave rather suddenly during the night."

Lainie sat up in bed, a deepening frown etched across her face. She didn't understand any of this. Alyse had told her that he wasn't supposed to leave for Nashville until this morning. She had wondered if he would even bother to say goodbye. Now she knew the answer. "Where did he go?"

"I don't know, dear. If you ask me, I think it was crazy of him to leave in the middle of the night. A body's got to get rest sometimes. Even his," she said smoothing out the wrinkles in Lainie's bed.

Lainie blinked, not at all convinced this wasn't just a dream. Her eyes skidded around the room while she tried to make some sense out of what the woman was saying.

"I don't understand...."

"It's quite simple, dear. He's gone, and I'm here to take care of you," Nurse Bell answered.

It couldn't be true. Lainie threw the covers aside, but Nurse Bell appeared immediately and grabbed hold of her arm.

"Now, dear, you know you can't get out of bed without my help. That's why I'm here."

"I need to get up. Help me, please," Lainie said anxiously, motioning with her hand toward the hallway. "His bedroom is to the left."

"All right, hold onto my arm, but I assure you, he's gone."

With help, Lainie managed to get to Zachary's room. Just what she expected—or even wanted—to find there, she didn't know. But she felt a need to lie across his bed, breathe the same air he had breathed, touch the same things he had touched—as though by doing so, she could accept the fact that he was gone.

Nurse Bell eased her onto his bed. Then, walking to the closet, the older woman pulled it open. "See, dear. His things are gone."

"Please," Lainie whispered, her throat almost too tight to speak. "I'd just like to be alone for a while. I'll call you when I'm ready to go back to my room."

The woman walked over to her and placed her arm around Lainie's shoulders. "I guess you're feeling you've lost them both, aren't you?"

Self-pity punched a huge hole in the last barrier holding back Lainie's tears. They began to roll down her pale cheeks.

She looked up and caught the faint glimmer of sympathy in her nurse's eyes just before the older woman turned and walked from the room, quietly shutting the door behind her.

"I wish I'd never heard of you, Zachary Benjamin," Lainie whispered, slamming her fist into the mattress. "And God, how I wish I'd never loved you."

She cried for a long time. Then, feeling drained of all emotion, she lay back and stared at the ceiling.

He'd looked so surprised last night when she'd told him about the phone calls she'd made to him. But surely it was all an act. She could still recall the words of his manager when he'd told her what Zachary had said about her and the baby. The poor man had sounded completely wretched at having to repeat them to her.

She rolled onto her side, and that was when she noticed an envelope with her name on it on the nightstand next to her. With trembling fingers, she reached for it, tore open the letter and began to read.

Lainie,
I've gone to Nashville to get some answers. I'll be in touch....

                                        Zachary

Her renewed tears tasted salty on her lips. A piercing ache gripped her heart. Despite everything, she still loved him, and she felt sorry... sorry for herself, for Zac and for their daughter, who, because of her mother's lie, would be going through her own private hell soon. How could something that happened so long ago have such a devastating effect on their lives today?

Somewhere between crying, probing her innermost feelings and slowly accepting her life for what it was, Lainie lost track of time. She didn't know how long she'd been in Zachary's room when she heard her daughter asking permission to enter.

Alyse came in and sat down next to her, a somber expression on her face. "It's time we talked, Mama."

A bittersweet smile touched Lainie's lips. Pulling herself erect, she sighed heavily. "Yes, I guess that time has finally come, hasn't it?" She met her daughter's gaze and found the courage she knew she would need in the minutes to follow.

She reached for her daughter's hand and squeezed it reassuringly. "You can ask me anything you'd like, and I promise to answer you truthfully."

Alyse lowered her head and stared at the hand holding hers. Unconsciously she touched the solitary gold band encircling the third finger of her mother's left hand. "Tell me about you and Daddy... and Zac."

Lainie took a deep breath and steadied her nerves. "What would you like to know?"

Alyse looked up, her eyes growing large and liquid. "Everything."

Fighting back her own tears, Lainie nodded. "All right. I'll tell you everything."

Her voice was shaky and weak as she began her story, starting with her first day at Harrington High, then moving on to her growing friendship with Cory and his wanting her to meet his older brother, Zac. As the story progressed, Lainie's carefully chosen words told the story of twenty years.

Constant tears spilled from Alyse's eyes, but she didn't interrupt her mother. With a strength she hadn't known she possessed, Lainie explained the last couple of days in a way that neither blamed nor exonerated Zachary—or herself. Only Cory remained as he had always been in her mind, a true and faithful friend whose undying love for his entire family had finally made him break his long-ago promise to her.

"And now," Lainie said, taking another deep breath and praying her daughter would somehow understand and yet knowing she probably wouldn't, "Zachary claims he never knew about you until your father told him only hours before he died. He says that if he had known, he would have come back to marry me."

She tightened her hold on her daughter's hand. "I can't tell you how sorry I am for never telling you before now, honey. I never wanted you to be hurt by my mistake," she continued, teardrops filling her dark eyes. "My single purpose in lying to you—and to everyone—was to protect you from being labeled Zachary Benjamin's illegitimate child. Can you imagine what the press would have done with a story like that? I couldn't let that happen. And no matter what you think of me, I want you to remember that Cory was a good father to you. He loved you very much. I love you, too."

"You know, it's funny," Alyse finally said, her voice barely above a whisper as she fought for self-control. "But I think I've always known. Maybe it was because of the gossip I heard from other people that was never mentioned in our house, or maybe it was because of the questions I'd asked that were never really answered. I don't know," she said, slowly shaking her head from side to side, "but I realize now I've always known there was something—some big secret that one day someone was going to share with me." She looked at her mother, tears streaming down her cheeks. "But the funny part is, I always pictured Daddy as the one telling me, not you." Suddenly bursting into sobs, she jumped from the bed and ran toward her room. "I'm sorry—I just have to be alone right now," she wailed as the door slammed shut behind her.

Although it was one of the toughest things she'd ever had to do, Lainie honored her daughter's request for privacy and stayed away. If there had been any way to change the past, to make it less painful for her child, she would gladly have paid any price to do so.

Hours later, as evening shadows promised the end of another day, she heard the door to Alyse's room squeak open. Her heart accelerated.

If only Cory were here, she told herself, he would have found a way to make everything right again.

And yet it was Zachary who she loved with a wild, passionate need that had enslaved her to him—even to this day. And while Cory's love had made her life good, her dreams of Zachary were what had kept her alive.

Had she really been living on dreams?

Turning her head toward the doorway, she caught her breath when she saw Alyse standing just inside the room, looking as lost and frightened as an orphan. "Oh, baby, I'm so sorry for everything," Lainie said, swallowing back a sob. "Come here."

Alyse didn't need any more encouragement. She rushed forward and threw herself into her mother's waiting arms. In the minutes that followed, they cried softly, rocking slowly back and forth to the tempo of their hearts.

Lainie remembered that someone had once said there was a time for all things on earth. For them, this was a time of healing.

As soon as he reached Nashville, Zachary went straight to the apartment he kept and telephoned Bobby Jones. Now he was anxiously awaiting the man's arrival. When the doorbell rang, he could hardly contain himself. Flexing his fingers in an attempt to release the tension building inside him, he walked to the door and opened it.

"Hey, son! It sure is great to have you back where you belong!" Bobby Jones exclaimed, stepping inside and slapping his client across the back. His round face was flushed. "What'cha say we pour ourselves a drink to celebrate?"

"Sure," Zachary replied, a slight edge to his voice. "Why not?"

Bobby helped himself to a drink with the familiarity of an old friend. He poured one for Zachary, too, splashing whiskey over the rim. He looked up and caught a glimpse of Zac's expressionless features. "Uh...sorry," he said, grabbing a cloth to wipe up the mess. Zachary didn't reply.

Bobby cleared his throat. "Well, were you able to do whatever it was you felt you had to do?" He laughed nervously. "You acted so strange when I called, I was beginning to think you weren't coming back."

Zachary sat down and watched as his friend fidgeted around the room. Obviously, something was bothering him. The gnawing ache in Zac's gut grew larger. Was it possible that Lainie was telling the truth? "Bobby, sometimes it becomes necessary for a man like me to rectify part of his past before he can go forward."

"You see what I mean? You're talking in riddles. You ain't never talked to me like that before."

"Something bothering you?"

Bobby gave a short laugh. "It's just you ain't making any sense, son," he said, gulping down the last of his drink. He walked to the bar and poured himself another shot of whiskey. Then he dabbed at the perspiration on his forehead with the white handkerchief he pulled from his coat pocket.

"Nervous, Bobby?"

"Yeah—sort of."

"We've known each other over twenty years. I don't recall you ever being nervous in my company," Zac said, never taking his steady gaze off the man. "Care to explain why that's suddenly changed?"

"I don't know what you mean. I'm just nervous. I'm always nervous. You know that."

"Not like this."

Bobby laughed again. "I saw Mona yesterday. She said you'd phoned her from Harrington to confirm on the benefit. Is that where you've been all this time?"

"Didn't you figure that out when you called me?"

"Nope...not really. I never dreamed you'd want to go back home. There ain't nothin' there for you."

Frowning, Zac held his whiskey glass near his lips. "I happen to think there is. As a matter of fact, I went back home for one reason. Revenge. The strange thing is, I heard a story that I still can't bring myself to believe."

Bobby's face turned ashen. Spreading his hands out in front of him, he said, "Now, wait a minute, son. I can explain. It ain't nothing like she told you."

Zachary rose slowly, his anger exploding within him. His narrowed eyes were like spears aimed at his old friend. "She who, Bobby?"

"Uhhh...you know—your brother's wife. What's her name?"

"Lainie."

"Yeah, that's her. She's a liar."

"Oh, yeah? Funny thing," Zac said. "That's exactly what she called me when I told her I'd never known she was pregnant with my baby. It's pretty clear that *some*body's lying."

"It ain't me, son. You got to believe me."

"She told me you'd offered to help her out of her predicament." Narrowing his eyes even more, Zac continued. "It makes me crazy to think you got away with your lies so easily. But we helped, didn't we? Lainie played right into your hands when she married my brother, and like the dumb country boy I was, I never suspected that you could've had anything to do with it."

"Okay, listen," Bobby said nervously. "Let's just calm down here so we can get a grip on things."

Zachary took a step toward him. "You've run out of time, Bobby."

"No, it ain't like that," Bobby said, wiping his hand across his mouth. "She's the one who's lying. I bet that kid ain't even yours."

"She's mine!"

"Look, I admit I did try to help her. I even offered to arrange an abortion for her so she wouldn't be stuck with the kid. But she didn't want nothin' to do with that."

Zac grabbed his manager by the shirt and yanked him up until his feet were almost off the floor. His face was mere inches from Zac's. "That was my baby you offered to get rid of. Mine," Zac said through clenched teeth. The next second he thrust the man away from him. "Get out of here before I lose control and rip you to shreds."

"Zac, son, listen to me. She was just trying to trap you—"

"She was pregnant with my child!" Zac yelled, his voice bouncing off the walls. "Can't you understand that? My baby. I loved her, and I would gladly have married her. Instead, my kid was raised by my brother because he and Lainie thought I didn't want her. You played God with my life! I never asked you to do that."

"Look," Bobby pleaded, "didn't she turn around and marry your brother at the drop of a hat? That proves she didn't care what man she had, as long as she had one. She was nothin' but a tramp."

Zac didn't even realize he had swung at the man until his fist smashed Bobby right between the eyes. The older man slumped to the floor, his hands flying up to cover the blood gushing from his face. "You broke my nose. You broke my nose!" he wailed.

Zac glared down at him. "Get out of here before I do worse."

Bobby Jones slid several feet away from the furious man towering over him. Slowly he staggered to his feet, blood dripping out between his fingers and staining the front of his pale yellow shirt. He headed for the door.

"You're through, Bobby. Don't you ever come near me or my family again, or so help me, you'll be sorry."

On Monday morning Alyse assured her mother she was doing fine as she packed and left for Houston. Lainie, however, wasn't convinced and worried about her all day. Not that she felt her daughter couldn't cope. But for now Lainie felt a need to mother her.

Nurse Bell was a tyrant. Actually, the woman was driving Lainie nuts. Hardheaded to a fault, she insisted on running things her way, like turning off the TV when she thought Lainie had watched enough, or drawing a bath when she thought her patient needed a soak—never mind that Lainie's skin was beginning to shrivel up.

Lainie was trying to contain her frustration. She hoped she would be capable of caring for herself by the end of the week—if she could last that long. She could then could tell Nurse Bell she wasn't needed, and the woman could either volunteer or be paid to boss someone else around.

In an attempt to put the past behind her, Lainie tried not to think of Zachary at all. He'd accomplished what he'd come home to do, and now he was gone. Their lives were once again worlds apart.

She should have been angry with him, she told herself, but somehow she couldn't find the strength. She had been wrapped up in her miserable anger for twenty years. She couldn't do it any longer. She simply didn't want to. Life was too short. Besides, she had been wrong about one thing. Zachary had suffered, too. There was no way he could have faked the raw emotion she'd seen on his face the last time they'd argued.

With the help of Nurse Bell, she had just settled herself in a chair in the parlor, her cast resting on the matching footstool, and was sipping on a tall glass of ice tea when she heard a car pull up to the house. Because of her cast, she remained seated and waited for Nurse Bell to get the door. But instead of using the front entrance, the visitor went to the back door and walked right in.

Then she heard Nurse Bell and the visitor exchange words. For a second she thought the voice sounded like Zachary's and her heart accelerated. Then she realized she was being foolish. Zachary was in Nashville, and thoughts of her were undoubtedly far from his mind.

From the heavy footsteps heading her way, she could tell the visitor was probably a man, though. Most likely Bryon, she quickly decided. He was always dropping by to see how she was doing.

But it wasn't Bryon's body that suddenly filled the doorway. Bryon wasn't nearly as tall, nor as broad shouldered, nor did he have the same earth-shattering effect on her as did the man standing before her.

"Hello, Lainie," Zac drawled.

Her breath caught in her throat. "What are you doing here?"

"I belong here. This is my home," he said quietly.

"But . . ." She was at a loss for words.

"We need to talk," he said.

Suddenly feeling very tired, she shook her head. "What more do you want from me? I've told Alyse that you're her father."

"I know."

Lainie's head jerked up to look at him. "You know?"

"She telephoned me late last night, and we spoke for a long time. She wanted to hear my side. Her feelings are pretty mixed up right now."

"Can you blame her?"

"I don't blame any of us. Not anymore. I confronted Bobby with what you told me. He finally admitted he'd lied to both of us."

Shocked, Lainie just stared at him. "He admitted it?"

Nodding, Zac took three long strides to reach her side. "That's right. He lied to you from the very beginning. He never gave me one of your messages. All he was doing was returning your calls and telling you I didn't want to have a thing to do with you or the baby, and all the while I didn't even know."

Lainie shook her head from side to side. "But why would he do something like that?"

"Because he figured if I got married, it would ruin the image of me he was trying to create for the public." Zac frowned. "He didn't want anyone or anything standing in my way."

Lainie stared at the floor for the longest time. "Does he have any idea what he's done to our lives?"

"He does now."

"Oh...God..." Lainie said with a sigh, her voice trembling with emotions. "Oh my God..."

She couldn't speak any longer.

"Please forgive me for all the suffering I've caused you," Zac said, kneeling at her side. He gathered her in his strong arms. "If you do, then it's over, Lainie. After twenty years, the pain will finally be over."

"I don't blame you, Zac. Not anymore."

He held her as she cried softly, whispering soft words of comfort, placing light kisses on her hair, her face. But the most comforting thing was simply being in his strong arms and not having to feel guilty about it.

Nurse Bell peeked in and smiled. She had packed earlier when Zachary had telephoned to say he was returning. Now she picked up her bag and let herself out of the house. Lainie was in good hands now—hands that were capable of healing her pain—and from the looks on their faces as they gazed at each other, it would be a long time before either of them even realized she was gone.

Zachary pulled several folded papers from his back pocket. "Here," he said, placing them in Lainie's lap.

She sniffed. "What's this?"

"I've deeded the house over to you. It's yours now. Consider it my wedding gift to you. I never gave you and Cory anything."

"But you can't do that."

"I most certainly can. I've talked it over with Alyse, and she agrees."

"But why?"

His features became thoughtful. "Because I love you, and I wanted to do something that would prove I was sorry about everything that's happened. I knew money wasn't the answer. This house is the only thing I have that means anything to you, so now it's yours."

"Oh, Zac," she said, struggling with her emotions. She gazed into his eyes and saw love shining in them. In that instant, she knew the house wasn't all she wanted. Without her first love sharing her days, the house would mean nothing to her. True, she and Cory had shared happiness here, but Cory was gone, though her memories of him would be with her always. Now it was time for making new memories, memories of her and Zachary and the happiness they'd earned. Somehow, Lainie knew it had been their destiny all along.

"I love you, Zac. I've always loved you."

He lifted her face in his big, warm hands and made her look into his eyes. "I know," he said. "Just as I've always loved you."

"This is going to be difficult for Alyse."

"She's confused right now, but she's trying very hard to sort everything out. She's strong. We just need to give her time."

Biting her bottom lip, she nodded.

"Do you remember how you kissed me the day I first left Harrington?"

Tears sparkled in her eyes. "Yes."

"Then kiss me like that now, only this time we'll be saying hello instead of goodbye."

"I never want to say goodbye again."

"We won't. Not once you become my wife."

Lainie lifted her face to his. "Do we dare dream again?"

"I never stopped, Lainie. Not for one single second." He pulled her into his embrace. "Just marry me, baby, and I'll show you what I mean for the rest of our lives."

Her lips met his as she whispered her answer.

Epilogue

One Year Later

The coliseum was packed. Lainie stood backstage and watched as the man she loved slipped the strap holding his guitar over his head and was transformed before her very eyes into the superstar his fans had come to see. Even after a year of traveling on the road with him, it still amazed her how he could be one man on stage and another off. She adored them both.

The voice of the lead guitarist filled the coliseum. "Okay, country music fans. The time has finally come for me to introduce the guy y'all've been waiting for. I'd like you to give a great big welcome to the one...the only...the superstar of country music...Zachary Benjamin."

A burst of applause and fans' screaming drowned out all other sounds. Zachary turned to Lainie and, while placing his hand on her protruding stomach, kissed her tenderly on the lips. Then, pressing his mouth to her ear, he whispered to her in his deep, throaty voice, "This one's for you and our baby."

Lainie grinned and pulled him near her. "You tell me that every time you go on stage."

"That's 'cause my whole life is devoted to you and our children. The three of you are everything to me."

Lainie smiled. "Did I tell you Alyse called today?"

He shook his head.

"Well, she and her new boyfriend—I think she said his name was Nick Davenport.... Anyway, she's been seeing him since she started singing with his band, and it must be getting pretty serious, because she wants us to meet him. They'll be coming home for the Fourth of July weekend."

Zachary grinned. "She's coming around, isn't she?"

"Yes," Lainie said, her heart constricting with the love she felt for him, for their beautiful daughter and for their unborn child.

He kissed her again then winked as his fans called impatiently for his appearance. He walked out, and as the spotlight found him, the crowd jumped to their feet in a deafening burst of applause. Zachary smiled, waved, and then bent down to shake hands with a few of the female fans who had succeeded in getting past security and now stood at the foot of the stage. Most of them held drooping flowers, stuffed animals, boots and album covers they hoped he'd take the time to autograph.

He stationed himself behind the microphone. "As always, this first song is dedicated to my lovely wife, Lainie."

The band began to play, and Zachary's voice came over the speakers. It was deep and throaty and sexy—and it turned Lainie's insides to jelly. At the age of forty, he still had a way of turning her on every bit as much as he had when he was nineteen. She couldn't wait until later that night when they would be back in their hotel room. The loving she knew he'd give her made a warm feeling spread through her body. Not even her pregnancy had interfered with their lovemaking. In fact, if possible, Zachary had become even more ardent, though he was always very gentle and conscious of her comfort. He had been at her side every step of the way and planned to be an active part of the actual birth. That pleased her a great deal. Though she had told him often, she felt sure he had no earthly idea how comforting his presence was going to be as she delivered their second child into the world. She made a mental note to tell him so again tonight.

She breathed a contented sigh. At long last she had found complete peace of mind. No more lies. Today every part of her being sang with the complete happiness she'd once thought was impossible for her and Zachary.

Her Zachary.

It sounded so right, and with a song in her heart, she knew it was.

From somewhere high above, her dear friend looked down on them and smiled. At last he could rest in peace, for all was right with the world below.

*   *   *   *   *

WRITTEN IN THE STARS

Travel along with
THE MAN FROM NATCHEZ
by Elizabeth August

When a lovely lady waves a red flag to tempt the Taurus man, will the bullheaded hunk charge into romance... or be as stubborn as ever? Find out in May in THE MAN FROM NATCHEZ by Elizabeth August... the fifth book in our Written in the Stars series!

Rough and rugged farmer Nate Hathaway wasn't about to let Stacy Jamison go it alone while searching for treasure in the Shenandoah Mountains! The man from Natchez was about to embark on a very tempting trip....

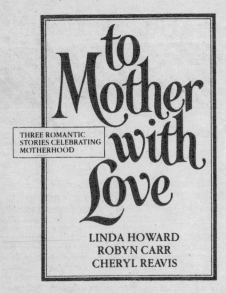
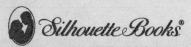